Teresa Burns Gunther

is an award-winning author whose fiction and nonfiction have been published widely in US and international literary journals and anthologies, including *New Millennium Writings*, *Mid-American Review*, *Alaska Quarterly Review*, *Everyday Fiction*, *The Doctor T. J. Eckleburg Review*, *Pure Slush*, *Best New Writing*, and many others.

Her stories have been recognized in numerous contests, including those at *Glimmer Train* and *Narrative*; her story "War Paint" was awarded the 52nd New Millennium Award for Fiction, 2022. An earlier version of this collection was a Finalist for the Orison Book Prize and the Hudson Prize.

Teresa is the founder of Lakeshore Writers Workshop where she leads workshops and classes and offers coaching and developmental editing services.

Learn more at www.teresaburnsgunther.com

HOLD OFF THE NIGHT

STORIES

TERESA BURNS GUNTHER

TRUTH SERUM PRESS

TRUTH SERUM PRESS

ISBN: 978-1-922427-00-7

BP#00117

Truth Serum Press
32 Meredith Street
Sefton Park SA 5083
Australia

Email: truthserumpress@live.com.au
Website: truthserumpress.net
Truth Serum Press catalogue: truthserumpress.net/catalogue

Cover design copyright © Matt Potter
Cover image copyright © FelixMittermeier
Author photograph copyright © Nan Phelps

Also available as an ePub eBook
ISBN: 978-1-922427-18-2
Also available as a Kindle eBook
ISBN: 978-1-922427-45-8

Truth Serum Press is a member of the
Bequem Publishing collective
bequempublishing.com

For Andy

Contents

Where Are You, Really?

Evelyn pulled into her garage, tires screeching on the concrete floor as she braked. Her bumper banged the twin bed frame her daughter had disassembled and dumped there. It teetered, then fell back against the tools hung on the pegboard wall. Her hands shook as she gripped and released the steering wheel.

"You're a damned liar, Carl." The garage door stuttered and groaned closed behind her. "Mommy track, my ass!"

The stink of exhaust fumes made her wonder about people who ended their misery in the garage. How many killed themselves over a job?

She trudged upstairs to her bedroom, stepped out of her skirt, and kicked it across the floor. Her new stockings snagged on her wedding ring as she pulled them off. She twisted them into a knot and flung them hard at the wall. They slid to the ground with a whisper.

The house was quiet with Christy at school and Hank in Paris on business. She pulled on a pair of Hank's soft plaid pajama bottoms. On her way downstairs, she paused in the door to Joshua's room, untouched. Just when he'd moved beyond the barbed-wire defense of adolescence, could joke with her, be himself again, he'd left. She thought about calling him, her boy, a freshman now at Emory, but he needed space and time to recalibrate the cord.

The answering machine flashed in the kitchen. She pushed Play. An automated voice droned: "This is the Attendance Desk at Washington High. Your child didn't report to school today. A written excuse will be required—" Evelyn raced back upstairs to find her sixteen-year-old still tangled up in sheets. Fear turned to fury.

"Christy! You're still in bed?"

Christy raised her blond head with its black roots and squinted at her mother. "Is that a trick question?" She checked her phone. "Shit!" She jumped up from the mattress lying on the floor in a sea of clothes, damp towels, and tangled cords.

"Why aren't you at school?"

"I overslept. Obviously."

"You say you're ready for more freedom but you can't even get yourself up for school."

Christy pushed past Evelyn, a morning snarl of a girl with a pierced nostril. "Could you make some coffee?"

"Yes ma'am," Evelyn said.

Christy stomped downstairs fifteen minutes later in flip-flops, sweatpants low on her hips, and a long-sleeved top that revealed a turquoise bra and too much of its contents.

"Is that what you're wearing to school?" Evelyn asked, forcing her eyes past the faint lines that scarred Christy's wrists. She topped up her coffee and poured a cup for Christy.

"Gosh. No. I'll wear my ball gown." A black thong peeked out over the back of Christy's pants as she bent to rummage through the fridge. She extracted chocolate milk, poured some into her coffee, and scrutinized Evelyn over her mug. "Is that what you're wearing?"

"Your underwear's showing," Evelyn said. The dark kohl around her daughter's eyes reminded her of the stuffed meerkat Christy had loved, couldn't sleep without. How many hours had Evelyn spent searching for it or sitting with Christy on her lap as it made its way through the wash cycle and dryer?

Christy waved her mug at Evelyn's lumpy clogs, Hank's pajama bottoms, and the sweater and pearls she'd worn to the office. "Like you aren't ridiculous?"

"Well, at least my boobs aren't hanging out for the world to see."

"Thank god for that," Christy mumbled. She slung her backpack over one shoulder and stood, hip jutting out. "You shoulda gone with Dad. You could be bombing around Paris and buying some clothes from this century."

"No. I could not." She couldn't leave Christy home alone. "I work, too." Evelyn wasn't about to tell her she was now unemployed.

"Yeah, but," Christy said, with that disdainful look that made Evelyn's hands clench.

"Yeah but what?"

Christy drained her mug and left it on the counter. "You're not exactly a real lawyer."

Evelyn pulled out bread to make a sandwich, then shoved the bread back in its bag. "You can make your own lunch," she said.

"Nah. I usually go off campus."

"Then why do I make lunches?"

Christy shrugged.

Evelyn pressed her hands into the counter's cool tile. She took a deep breath. "For your information I passed the bar twelve years ago. In the state of California, that makes me a lawyer."

"Yeah, for dead people. You're not like Dad, you don't go to court."

"I work with the firm's top clients. They're there because of me." She poked her finger into the counter as she spoke, repeating her argument to her boss that morning.

"God, don't be so touchy."

Evelyn was too furious to speak. Did other mothers long to slap their daughters?

"Well?" Christy said.

"Well, what?"

"Aren't you driving me?"

Evelyn crossed her arms. "Are you sure you want to be seen with someone so ridiculous?" She hadn't meant to raise her voice.

"C'mon, Mom!"

Evelyn shook her head. "I think you walking will do us both some good."

"Well, could you at least write me a note?"

Evelyn tore a sheet of paper off the pad by the phone and wrote *Please excuse Christy's tardiness—she was too irresponsible to get up on time.* She signed it, *Mother Evelyn.* Christy stuffed it into her backpack without reading it and strode to the door.

"Will you be home for supper?"

"No," Christy said. She flung the door wide. "I'll probably be dead since I have to hitchhike and some perv will rape me, slit my throat and toss me in a ditch."

"Okay," Evelyn said with a tight smile. "Have a nice time."

Christy banged the door shut, rattling the windows. Evelyn unclasped her pearls and clutched them hard in her hand. Christy wouldn't hitchhike. Outside, she sidestepped the newspaper, texting as she walked, no doubt an SOS for a ride. Evelyn slumped down in a kitchen chair. A good mother would have woken Christy—but Evelyn left early, and Hank insisted the kids be responsible for their own schedules. "If they can program a cell phone," he said, "they can set an alarm." He would be in Paris for three more days. She missed him and hated his new assignment, an international copyright case involving an American record producer and a popular French band. She couldn't remember the name, but Christy said they were "straight fire." Christy was easier on Hank; he was more patient with her, though he'd have had a fit about her outfit.

Evelyn spent the rest of the morning cleaning, pulled the kitchen curtains down and threw them in the wash. Her housekeeper was coming in two days, but she was mad with energy. *Ridiculous* echoed in her ears as she sat before her computer to update her resumé. She was distracted by a Golden Lab outside, straining at its leash, barking at the squirrels racing up and down her oak tree. Who would hire her now? At her age?

She walked out for the paper. Her front yard had once been a gathering place for the neighborhood kids. She looked up through the oak's branches at the tree fort and was filled with something like grief for the days when her children were small and sweet, and it was easy for them to love her. She tugged on the fort's rope and the ladder unfolded, shaky and urgent, like her children's hands. The house phone rang.

The machine picked up before she stepped inside. A sound like drumming fingers filled the speaker.

"Evelyn?" It was Carl. Her boss. Ex-boss.

She grabbed the phone. "I'm here," she said, certain he'd changed his mind.

"Oh, Evelyn." She hated his patronizing tone. "You weren't in your office," he said. "You didn't answer your cell. Janine said you left."

"I gave my notice, remember?" He didn't respond. "What do you want, Carl?"

"I want to be sure you're okay."

"Why? Afraid I'm in my car with an exhaust hose through my window?"

"Oh, Evelyn." He chuckled. "You have such an ... odd sense of humor."

"Actually, I'd prefer a swan dive off the west side of the Golden Gate at sunset."

He coughed. "Are you okay?"

"I was just denied partner. For the second time. How would you be?" She paced, pounding her fist into her hip, her clogs slapping against the floor.

"Well, I didn't say never."

"But you didn't say now."

Silence. That drumming again. "Evelyn, you need to be patient. These are tough times."

"I've been patient."

"You're disappointed, but don't be rash."

Evelyn opened her mouth but thought better of speaking. "I have to go." She hung the phone back in its cradle, lifted it, and slammed it down again. She dug her cell phone out of her purse. A message from Carl, but Hank still hadn't called. She tucked it in her pocket and pulled chicken from the freezer, then put it back. Even if Christy came home, she'd probably bail on dinner at the last minute with the excuse of a 3:00 lunch or one more friend in a love crisis. "Mom," she'd say, "that's what friends do." As if Evelyn hadn't a clue about sacrifice. As if she had nothing better to do than cook for an empty house. It was 1:30. She wondered if Christy even went to school. The house suddenly felt too hot and close. She threw open the front door and saw the tree fort ladder she'd left down, so rattled by Carl's phone call that she'd forgotten. She grabbed a baguette from the kitchen counter, a dusty bottle of red from the wine rack.

Baguette under one arm, bottle in hand, she climbed the treehouse ladder's rickety rungs; it tilted and swayed. She froze, clutched the rough wood with her free hand, and looked down at the dizzying carpet of grass. Climbing more slowly, she reached the top rung and set the wine and bread inside, then drew herself up on one knee. One of her clogs crashed down the ladder and banged against the trunk.

The tree house's old carpet was littered with acorns and sharp leaves. Her breath quickened from the inrush of panic she'd tried to bury in housework. She hoisted the ladder up and hugged her knees. "Stop it!" she hissed.

She'd made the decision—profession second, motherhood first. "Look where that got me!" she yelled. A squirrel paused its chittering and cocked its head at her. "I know," she said. "I'm ridiculous." In law school, when she found herself pregnant with Joshua, five years earlier than planned, she'd carried on under the Superwoman myth that it was possible to have it all. Then, at six months, she was put on bed rest. Christy came along two years later, and she lost momentum, postponing her dream of becoming a litigator. Still, she continued going to school part time, passed the bar and was quickly hired as an associate. She loved the complexity of environmental law, longed to do work that might temper human's destructive activity with the increasingly vulnerable parts of the planet. But she felt torn, sad that the nanny took her babies to

Mommy-Baby Gymboree and T-ball, heartbroken to miss the second farmer's dance in the school play. Eventually, she transferred to Estates and Trusts, and was happy in a second-string kind of way.

Encircled by the gray plywood walls, she rocked and focused on breathing until her panic eased. The smell of the wood took her back as did Christy's old blanket on the floor, Holly Hobbie's image now barely visible. How many times had Christy curled with that blanket in Evelyn's arms?

She scooted across the floor and leaned into a ratty pillow propped against the tree's rough bark. She looked up through the roof's Plexiglas skylight to the higher branches. She hadn't been in the fort since the kids were little, when they'd insisted she join in their games. Joshua would climb the tree, showing off, terrifying her as Christy clapped in delight, and Evelyn had marveled at her primal, irrational love for them.

Something dug into her back. Behind the pillow, she found three empty beer cans—one filled with ashes, the others crushed—and a rusty Altoids box she opened to find matches and two neatly rolled joints. She clutched the box in her hands and read the graffiti on the walls: names of people she didn't know, *69, pow, F-U-C-K*, hearts circling initials she scanned her brain to match with names and faces. And in Christy's cursive: *Mom = bitch.*

Evelyn felt the thumping threat of panic again. She lifted one of the joints, sniffed its pungent aroma. Wasn't it her duty to confiscate it? The match hissed with the first strike. She inhaled too quickly and burst into a coughing fit. Her brother had told her today's pot was ten times stronger than the weed they'd smoked as kids. She tried to relax. Her jaw hurt. She took another hit, slower, and imagined a swirling fog cottoning her dread.

Sunlight fell on a candle in the corner; something red glittered beside it. She crawled on all fours and found condom packets two years past their expiration date. She sincerely hoped they were Joshua's. Had Christy had sex? It pained her to think of it. Would Christy tell her if she asked? Evelyn had never talked about sex with her own mother who'd found "that kind of talk" distasteful.

The first time Evelyn had sex—in Art Belcher's dad's truck with Paradise Gardens stenciled on the side—she was sixteen, Christy's age. Art laid a sleeping bag in the dirty truck bed, which smelled of fertilizer. For months after, she carried the secret of her transformation inside her, terrified her mother would read it in her face yet wanting so much to tell her.

She and Hank had a good sex life or would if he were ever home. They'd tried phone sex but were always in different time zones, working different schedules, and it just left her feeling alone. She wondered what became of Art Belcher, a goofy kid who hid behind his lank hair, a habit she'd mistakenly thought mysterious. She laughed. A bird answered.

Her cell phone rang. Joshua.

She fumbled to answer. "Hi, honey! I'm so happy you called. How are you?"

"Well, my graphing calculator broke. I need a new one." He recited a brand name followed by a string of letters and numbers. She giggled.

"What's so funny?" he asked.

"Sounds like Greek."

"Get a pen so you can write it down."

But Evelyn was tired of taking orders. "Why?"

"So you can send it to me."

"Can't you get one at the bookstore? That's what your credit card is for, academic emergencies."

"They don't have the right one."

"Did you try to order it online?" He was silent. "Do you really need my help, Joshua?"

"Nah, I guess not. Math just sucks. What are you doing?"

Evelyn looked at the joint sleeping on one of the flattened beer cans. "Research."

"Yeah?"

"Yes indeedy, pretty powerful material." This made her giggle again.

"Mom?"

She tried to stop.

"Mom!"

"Yes," she gasped. "I'm here."

"Are you okay?"

"I'm fine." She imagined his shrug and felt a sharp pang. She sat up straight. "Actually, not so great. I didn't make partner."

"Oh man. That's a bummer."

"Yeah." When he didn't say more, she asked if his new roommate was working out better.

"I guess." His voice was too soft to be convincing.

"You sure? I hope—"

"Yeah, I know." He cleared his throat. "I better get to class."

"I love you, Joshua."

"Yeah. Me too."

Then he was gone, leaving her with the ache of missing him. Did he feel it too? Had she missed something in his call and let him down? Was he homesick? Her guilt was interrupted by a flash of irritation. He hadn't seemed to care that she didn't make partner. Was it unreasonable to want her kids to care about her life?

She lay back, so weary, mesmerized by the shifting leaves.

A buzzing woke her. She was confused for a moment. Her watch read 3:15. She picked up her phone. Hank.

"I didn't get it," she said without preliminaries.

"You're kidding!"

"I wish." She suddenly remembered the night before, choosing her outfit for her performance review, something that announced *Partner*, Christy leaning in the doorway, watching. "Mom," she said, her nose ring flaring. "It must suck getting old."

"Evelyn?"

"I'm here, Hank. I miss you."

"I miss you too. How're you doing?"

"Wishing I had a certain man here to sex me up and love me, take my mind off my failures, get my daughter off my back." She studied the cobwebbed corners of the roof.

"Is she okay?" he asked in the tone they used when they talked about her.

"How can I tell?"

He sighed. "Remember what they said, keep your eye on the trend? She *is* better."

But Evelyn didn't want to revisit that grief.

"I can't believe you didn't make partner," he said.

"Me, too."

"Where are you?"

"Nature center."

"Pardon?"

"Up a tree." She wiped her eyes. "And according to Christy, ridiculous. Oh, I found her pot. Good stuff by the way."

Hank was silent for a moment. "What's going on?"

Evelyn laughed.

"Should I be concerned?"

"Why? Isn't it nice to hear someone laughing? Especially someone who's taken for granted and treated like shit?"

"Not when she's my wife, and upset, hiding out and smoking dope. And when did Christy start smoking dope? Why don't I know about it?"

"Maybe because you're never here?"

At his irritated snort, she ended the call. She'd never hung up on him before.

She lit the joint again and blew smoke rings, feeling an irrational pride that she still knew how. The smoke wove up around the trunk and she knew she was truly seeing the tree and loving it for the first time. She slid up against it, put her ear to its rough skin, listening for a heartbeat. Where had that come from, that idea of a heart at a tree's core? When Hank and his brother built the treefort, she'd banned matches. Obviously, no one listened. She lit the candle and wondered if she'd ever done anything that made any difference at all. The phone rang again.

"Evelyn?"

"'Tis I," she said, imagining Hank's exasperation, his dark eyes cast upward. She tore a hunk off the baguette with her teeth and chewed, eyes closed, savoring the doughy pleasure. She was ravenous.

"Evelyn? Where are you?"

"Whoa." She swallowed. "That's just it."

"What's it?"

"I don't know where I am." Evelyn rolled bread into tight balls of dough, fighting back tears. "I only know that I've wasted my life."

"Jesus Christ, Evelyn."

"Listen. I'm a failure as a mother."

"That's not true."

"I feel like a fool. Carl hugged me, patted my back like I'm some sorry old broad. I should've slugged him." She laughed, imagining her fist connecting with Carl's tanned jaw.

"He touched you? What's his excuse for stupid?"

"It wasn't sexual. Maybe if he'd made a pass it would be easier."

"Jesus, Evelyn."

"Why do you keep invoking Christ?" She wanted to hate Hank, top of his game, irreplaceable, senior partner. When Christy was arrested, he'd swooped in, Superdad, but it was Evelyn who was left to work out the day-to-day pieces. She felt like screaming, then reminded herself she was very stoned. And unbearably thirsty. "Hang on." She put the phone on speaker and set it down.

Hank made a humming noise, probably reading his email. She twisted open the bottle, took a swig of the dark red wine and smacked her lips. It was delicious. "You and me, sister." She raised the bottle to the tree. A boy had once called her a stone fox. "Ha!" She tugged the PJ bottoms down to her ankles and studied her long legs, gone pale and softer now.

"What?" Hank's voice was far away. "Evelyn?"

"Yeah?"

"What happened with Christy?"

"After I quit—"

"You quit?"

"I had to." She took the phone off speaker and held it to her ear. "I came home and there was a message from school that she didn't show up. So, of course, I thought the worst, but I found her in bed, still asleep. She took her sweet time getting dressed and you would not have liked her outfit—very slutty. I'm so tired of her nastiness, always having to tiptoe around her moods. I work my ass off for our family, for my idiot boss, but I get no respect. People treat me like I'm a joke." She ran her finger across the graffiti on the wall.

"Where are you, really?" he asked.

"An arboreal bar." She drank from the bottle and wiped her mouth. "On my way to wasted."

"Babe, you're worrying me."

"Well, don't listen." She hung up, tossed the phone aside and chugged the wine.

The front door of the house banged, startling her. She yanked her bottoms back up. The tree stood large, shading the yard, the fort level with the second floor. She could see into Christy's room and the master bedroom; what had Joshua and Christy seen? Christy's door swung open. Evelyn watched her strip off her top and smell her armpits. There was something on her back. Evelyn strained to see. A tattoo? Christy picked a hoodie off the floor, sniffed it, and zipped it on as she wandered out of her room, reappearing in Evelyn's. She opened Evelyn's jewelry box, peered in, let it fall shut then opened the top dresser drawer. Evelyn's heart sank as she watched her daughter slip money from her emergency stash.

A car honked at the curb. Christy flew out of the house a moment later. Her flip-flops snapped as she hurried down the path under the tree to the street where she hopped into an unfamiliar Honda Civic with dark windows. It sped off. A burst of wind worried the treetop, knocked the candle on its side. Evelyn picked it up and let the hot wax drip into her palm.

The neighbor's lights were turning on. Her own house sat dark and silent. It was almost five o'clock, but she wasn't ready to go in. She played with the wax, wondering where Christy was going, fighting her mind's incessant detour to catastrophe. What would it take to trust that her daughter was going to be okay?

Twenty minutes later, another car pulled to the curb. Evelyn wrapped the Holly Hobbie blanket around her shoulders and looked out to see her boss emerge from a Porsche Carrera. Yeah, Carl. Times are real tough. He walked under the tree and knocked on the door. What was he doing? Couldn't she have any peace? She fingered an acorn, dying to chuck it at him. He knocked again, rang the bell. It echoed in her empty house as the Honda Civic screeched up to the driveway. Had the fender been bashed when it left? They hadn't been gone long. What was Christy up to? Buying drugs? The car door opened; AC/DC rioted the air. Christy climbed out, exchanging monosyllabic grunts with the driver that reminded Evelyn of the texts Christy sent: *k, ltr,* and *lol*—to which Evelyn first responded *lots of love to you, too! xo*, and Christy quickly texted back: *Doh! lol = laff out loud.* The car sped off and Christy stood, running the zipper of her hoodie up and down, revealing her turquoise bra. Shoulders slumped, she turned to the house and Evelyn understood with a pang that something had happened, with a boy or at school and Christy now believed herself doomed. She stopped when she saw Carl.

"Can I help you?" Christy asked like a well-brought-up child.

Carl stepped off the porch with a salesman's smile, his hand thrust out. "I'm Carl, your mother's boss."

Christy looked at the dark house. "I don't think she's here." She flicked her hair off her shoulder and crossed her arms under her breasts. Evelyn cringed hoping Carl's view wasn't as advantageous as her own.

"Are you sure?" he asked, sliding his unshaken hand into his pocket.

"You can search the house if you think I'm lying," Christy snapped.

Evelyn grinned.

"No, no," he said with his condescending laugh. "Just tell her I came by. I'd like to talk to her."

"I bet you would." She looked him up and down.

"Well, nice to see you." Carl had to step around her to get by.

"Don't fuck with my mom."

"Pardon?" he said, pulling his chin into his neck.

"She's got more brains in her left foot than you have in your whole fucking ancestral tree."

Evelyn's jaw dropped. Christy followed Carl to his car, hands on hips, thong peeking out as Carl strapped himself in then peeled off down the street. Christy walked slowly to the house. Evelyn watched for her to reappear at the front door, but the tree fort trembled, the ladder unfolded, and Christy hurried up the ladder, tears spilling down her cheeks. She spotted Evelyn and screamed. "Fuck! Mom?"

"What?" Evelyn cried, startled.

"What are you doing here?"

"What do you care?" Evelyn sniffed and relit the candle. It was dark now in the fort.

Christy put her hand on her heart; candlelight flickered on her face. "You scared me."

It hurt to see the lines that scarred her daughter, though fainter now. Christy saw her staring and pulled down her sleeves, clutched the cuffs in her fists. Evelyn tensed, anticipating nastiness but Christy sat and hugged her knees, rubbed her tears on her sweats, leaving dark smudges under her eyes that took in the remains of the baguette, the bottle of wine.

"Did you have a bad day, honey?" she asked, mimicking Evelyn with a watery smile.

"Yes," Evelyn said.

"Because of your job?"

Evelyn leaned back against the pillow, surprised by her daughter's unguarded face; it had been so long since she'd seen it. "How do you know about that?"

"Dad texted me."

Evelyn gave this a moment's thought.

"Mom, that's unfair."

"Yes, it is. But so is having a husband so far away when I need him. And a daughter who says such hurtful things."

Christy wove her fingers through her toes and avoided Evelyn's eyes. "You shouldn't take everything so personal."

"It is personal. It's my life."

Christy's fingers clenched. Her eyes lit on the joint and flattened beer can and widened. "Mom? Did you smoke?"

"O.M.G.," Evelyn said, her voice flat.

Christy grinned. "Did you hear what I said to Carl?"

"I did."

The wind blew. Evelyn hugged the blanket close. The tree creaked and swayed. A good mother would have faith, get a grip, ask about the stealing, the pot and condoms, the dented Honda Civic, and what she hoped, but doubted, was a henna tattoo. She looked up into the old oak, its branches bold and sturdy, reaching out to hold off the night.

"Christy," she said, and opened the blanket wide.

Lilies

Jennifer walked head down into a biting wind that pulled at her hair and whistled in her ears. She jumped, startled, when a squirrel zigzagged across her path. She concentrated on the cracks—*break your mother's back*—in the sidewalk. It wasn't until she turned the corner and saw her apartment building, blinding white in the electric sky, that she remembered. She searched her pockets and purse and realized she'd left her phone at work.

She pushed at her door—3G—and it pushed back. She conjured an intruder on the other side, but it was just a manila envelope wedged underneath. She yanked it out, ripping the corner, hurried inside, grabbed her landline, and dialed.

"Pick up," she whispered, her door still ajar.

"Happy Trails Preschool, Kelly speaking." The talk and laughter of children in the background accompanied the greeting.

"Kelly, I forgot to tell you—achoo!" Jennifer sneezed again, blew her nose.

"You sound terrible!"

"That's why I left. Listen, there's a change in pickup for Elise. It's a delicate situation." Jennifer twisted the old phone's cord. "The babysitter had an emergency. Elise's father called to say he'd pick her up. Since their divorce we're supposed to check with her mother first, but she's out of town and I couldn't reach—"

"You worry too much," Kelly said.

Jennifer pursed her lips. She was just doing her job. "Who's the dad?"

"Dr. Benson. Green eyes, dark hair, like Elise."

"Ah! The one you have a crush on!" Kelly teased.

"What?" Jennifer regretted telling her about meeting Dr. Benson at school. How he'd made her tongue-tied, so handsome in his cashmere sweater and neatly trimmed beard, leaning close to touch her arm as he spoke. She ran a thumb across her lips, remembering her buzzing excitement.

"I hate to ask," Kelly said, "but can you take Templeton?"

Templeton, the school pet, a rat, gave Jennifer the willies with its hairless tail and quivering whiskers. She shrugged out of her coat. "I thought you were taking him."

"I'm going to meet Michael's parents," Kelly said. She was Jennifer's best friend, but when she met Michael on HeavenMadeMatches.com Jennifer felt abandoned. Kelly wanted her to try the site, but it seemed desperate. Besides, Kelly had met some real creeps. "I can drop him off— Max, we don't put crayons up our nose—um, is that okay? I'll bring your phone, you left it here."

Jennifer had hoped for better company over the long weekend. "I guess," she said. It wasn't like she was going anywhere.

"Thanks," Kelly said. "Feel better."

"Have a fun weekend," Jennifer said with an enthusiasm she didn't feel but Kelly was already gone.

Her head ached, but she was out of ibuprofen. She found her thermometer, slid it under her tongue, and shuffled into the kitchen to her refrigerator, covered with handmade magnets and children's works of art. The frigid air cooled her face. She longed for juice but found only a wrinkled apple, ranch dressing, and a wedge of suspect cheese. Working the thermometer in her mouth, she leaned against her counter and surveyed her apartment with pleasure. A present to herself on her twenty-fifth birthday, the result of three careful years of planning and saving. A red light blinked on her answering machine; she pushed Play, then Stop when she heard her mother's voice. Her mother had begged her to get a roommate, but Jennifer didn't want to live with a stranger; she loved living alone.

She raised the blinds in her living room and crooked her head to see Mount Rainier; the thermometer tapped the glass. She slumped into her sofa. The torn manila envelope spilled newspaper clippings and scribbled notes. Her mother's red inked command—*Read This!*—topped a clipping about cancer rates in single women. Jennifer stuffed it all back in and tossed it aside. The thermometer read 100.1. The phone rang; she let the machine answer.

"Jennifer." Her mother's wheedling voice was punctuated by the brisk tapping of heels. "Your name is still on your message, that's not safe. And don't forget to get your flu—" The machine cut her off. Jennifer's intercom squawked, startling her. She hopped to her feet. The room spun. She steadied herself on the wall and said "Kelly?" through the intercom.

"Miss Jones?"

"Yes?"

"It's Jerry Benson. Elise and I have something for you." Jennifer wondered what Kelly had said. Or was this her idea of a joke?

"I'll have to come down. My buzzer's broken." She kept forgetting to ask her landlord to fix it, though her mother reminded her daily, *What if you need the police?* Jennifer quickly combed her hair, tried to conceal her red nose, and dabbed on lipstick.

Stepping out of the elevator, she saw a dark shape through the watered glass of the building's foyer. It was Dr. Benson with his neat beard, cage in hand. He towered over Elise, who peeked out from behind him.

"Hello, Elise," she said.

"Surprise, Miss Jennifer," the child said in her small, serious voice. Outside the sky had darkened. Jennifer pulled the door wider.

"Do you remember me?" Dr. Benson asked with a smile. The green of his tweed jacket matched his eyes.

"Yes, of course." She felt herself blush. Worried she might be spreading germs, but not wanting to refuse him, she shook his large hand.

He lifted the cage. "Special delivery."

"Thank you, Dr. Benson."

"Jerry. Please." Was he saying please about his name or about coming in? Her confusion was lost in a string of violent sneezes. He looked alarmed as she took a staggering step toward the cage.

"Oh ... dizzy," she said.

"Let me help you with this."

"Thank you." Her voice sounded far away. She worked her jaw to open her ears. Dr. Benson took her elbow and held the elevator door with his foot as she stepped inside.

"Come, Elise," he said but the girl stared at the thick black padding that draped the walls. She twisted her body, right and left, hair swinging, blue skirt twirling at her waist.

Jennifer slipped into her singsong teacher voice. "Someone's moving in. They put these up so nothing gets hurt."

Elise eyed the padded walls warily, but finally stepped inside before the elevator slid shut. Up they went, joined together in the mirrored doors. Elise made faces at her reflection. Templeton skittered in his cage. Jennifer examined her slacks and turtleneck, her pale face. A Mrs. Potato Head, she thought, her features representing a convergence of all the oddities of her family tree. How she wished she'd inherited her mother's beauty; her own eyes were large but her mouth too wide for her narrow nose. Her ears, hidden beneath her straight dirty-blond hair, had once earned her the playground nickname 'Dumbo'.

Dr. Benson cleared his throat. "I overheard the other teacher—"

"Miss Kelly," Elise interjected.

"—saying the rat—"

"Templeton—"

"Elise. Don't interrupt," Dr. Benson said. "Anyway ..." He seemed for a moment to have lost his place. "I offered to drop it off." Jennifer wondered why. The doors slid open.

"I hope I'm not contagious," Jennifer said.

"Don't worry," Dr. Benson said and smiled. He followed her with the rat down the carpeted hall. Elise slipped her hand into Jennifer's.

"What kind of medicine do you practice, Dr. Benson?" She'd slipped into her singsong voice again, a bad habit when she was nervous.

"Psychiatry."

"Really?" She could hear her mother sniff. *Shrinks: crazy makers, money pits.*

Jennifer opened her door. Elise explored the living room, touching things, testing the chintz sofa for its bounce, dipping her fingers into the small fountain that sparkled in the window's fading light.

"Where would you like it?" Dr. Benson asked, hoisting the cage.

At Kelly's house, she thought, but removed a cushion from the window seat. The rat peered through the bars, nose twitching. Jennifer shivered, turned her back.

"Are you okay?" he asked. "Is there someone to take care of you?" Elise peeked into Jennifer's bedroom. "A family member?" He jerked his chin, and Elise scurried back to his side. "A friend or neighbor?"

"My best friend's meeting her boyfriend's parents this weekend." Jennifer shrugged. The closest thing she'd had to a serious boyfriend was George when she still lived at home. She'd kept him a secret from her parents the whole nine months but in the end, he said he saw himself with a more ambitious woman. His friends kept telling him she was great, she's so good with kids, but George didn't really like children. He figured he'd have one or two—it's what one does—but he didn't want to make a life of it.

Dr. Benson coughed.

"They're pretty serious," Jennifer told him. "You know how it is." He raised his eyebrows, and she choked back a lick of laughter. "I'll be fine. It's just a cold." She crossed her arms, embarrassed. "Aspirin and rest, that's all I need."

"Who lives here?" Elise asked.

"Just Miss Jennifer," her father said, surveying the apartment. "Colorful." He pointed to the red coffee table and floor-to-ceiling shelves painted a golden yellow, filled with novels, children's picture books, and how-to books on arts and crafts. She cringed at the self-help books with bold titles like *Embracing Fear* and *Find the Courage to Live*.

"No! She lives at my school!" Elise frowned at Jennifer as if she'd caught her in a lie. She ran to the window seat and whispered into the cage. "She doesn't live here. She lives at Happy Trails!"

Jennifer gave her a quick, reassuring smile and sat on the edge of the sofa. The rat raced on its wheel, making an annoying squeak.

"Elise. Don't be silly," Dr. Benson said. He noticed an easel turned to the wall. "What's this?"

"Oh, that? Just a painting. It's not finished."

"May I?" he asked.

Jennifer never showed her paintings to anyone, but without thinking said, "Okay."

Dr. Benson carefully spun the easel and pulled off the drape. His eyes traveled the still life's three stark white lilies, stiff in a too-small vase against a background of purples and greens. Their opaque-eyed faces stared out. Jennifer studied the swirl of confused color emerging from the bottom, she wasn't sure yet what it was trying to be.

"You made flower faces!" Elise said and wrinkled her nose. "Ew, they have knives stuck in."

Jennifer leaned closer, amazed to see that the petals did look like knives stuck into the head of one of the lilies. She twisted a throw pillow back and forth in her hands.

"Interesting." Dr. Benson rocked on his heels, hands in pockets. "What do you call it?"

"Garden Party." It just popped out. The painting had no name yet.

"So, a teacher and an artist," he said.

She shook her head, uncomfortable. He opened his mouth to say something, but the phone rang. He offered to get it as her outgoing message filled the room. *Hello. This is Jennifer. Sorry I missed your call. Please leave a message.* So dull. So unlike Kelly's message with its snappy music and her cat meowing goodbye.

"Honey? Are you there?"

Jennifer flinched.

"Did the package arrive?" Her mother paused, her exhale loud in the phone before the machine clicked off.

"My mother thinks I should paint pretty pictures to make people happy."

Dr. Benson frowned.

"She thinks my paintings are dark and angry." Feeling exposed, Jennifer draped the easel. Her head felt like it would split in two. "Do you have any Advil?" she asked. "I'm out."

"No," Dr. Benson said. "I can go get you some."

"Oh, no!" she said. "I couldn't ask you to do that."

"You didn't. It's no trouble. I insist. Doctor's orders," he said with mock sternness.

"Well, thank you."

"Daddy, what about our special vacation?" Elise asked.

"Special is helping people when they're sick," he said, and turned to Jennifer. "May I tell you something?"

She nodded, feverish.

"Going through my divorce was a constant litany of what's wrong with me. It's nice to do something for a woman who appreciates kindness." He took Elise's hand and pointed to Jennifer's keys. "We'll take these, so you won't have to come downstairs again."

The door clicked shut behind them. She put her feet on the table, admiring her new high-top tennies, a vast improvement over the crepe-soled everydays her mother bought her. She closed her eyes and heard her mother saying, *You let him take your keys! He has a beard; he must be hiding something!* And she laughed.

He returned with a grocery bag, Elise followed him to the kitchen, cradling a paper cone.

"This is so nice of you," Jennifer called to him, struggling into an upright position. She tucked her hair behind her ears then quickly fluffed it out again. "I'm not usually so helpless."

"I don't think you're helpless," he called back.

"I do," Elise whispered from the kitchen doorway, staring down at her shoes.

"Your father's very kind," Jennifer said, surprised by the girl's sudden boldness.

Dr. Benson carried a vase of flowers from the kitchen and set it on the red coffee table. Jennifer inhaled sharply at the sight of the white lilies, like the ones in her painting. But these were so fragrant, so alive, just beginning to open.

Elise frowned. "Are those for Miss Jennifer?" she asked, in a pouty voice.

His look silenced her. "Elise, let's get those grapes for the rat," he said, and muttered something about a divorce being hard as he pulled his daughter into the kitchen. Jennifer heard him talking but couldn't make out his words. He returned a moment later with a glass of water and laid four pills in her hand. "Take these," he said, and handed her the glass.

"What are they?"

He looked hurt by her question. "Ibuprofen," he said. "And something for your cold."

Jennifer took the first pills and considered the others. He nodded. He was a doctor. She swallowed them and thought she should call her mother. He returned to the kitchen. It sounded like he was searching through her cupboards then she heard her kettle whistle. A moment later he brought her a cup of tea.

"You must be very good at what you do," she said, and felt a bead of sweat slide down between her breasts.

Elise walked in clutching purple grapes in her cupped hands. "Mommy said he's infectual," she said.

"Ineffectual," Dr. Benson corrected. The corners of his mouth drooped. "She did?"

"What's that mean?" Elise asked.

"It means that your mother has hostility issues." His shoes clicked on the floor as he walked to the window, hands behind his back. "Carol's one of those women," he said, "incapable of appreciating a caring man."

Elise was busy whispering to Templeton and feeding him grapes. Jennifer hoped she hadn't heard. She wanted to tell Dr. Benson to look the other way to see the mountains, but suddenly it was an effort to form words. Besides, he was probably anxious to go. She pushed herself up as Elise released the rat from his cage.

"Don't," she said. Dizzy again she grabbed the couch.

"Oh dear," he said. "Let's get you to bed."

"Let's?" Jennifer said.

He nodded, as if they'd reached an agreement. Suddenly his presence felt wrong. She didn't really know him.

"You should go," she said, but her blood rushed to her feet and the room turned around and round.

She woke in her darkened bedroom and heard someone talking. "Who's there?" Her voice was a cracked whisper. Her throat felt raw. She was hot from sleeping in her clothes. She opened her door to find Dr. Benson sitting on her couch, talking on his cell phone. "What's going on?" she asked, surprised to find him there.

"You shouldn't be out of bed." He slipped his phone into his pocket and popped to his feet.

Jennifer groped her way along the bookshelves to her kitchen and the refrigerator humming in its arched alcove. It was full of food. There was fresh orange juice and a basket of ripe red strawberries she didn't remember buying.

"Let me," he said. He took the juice from her shaking hands, held her elbow, and led her to the couch. Elise was crouched in a cave she'd constructed with cushions and pillows. She peered out at them as she sang softly to Templeton, "The itsy-bitsy spider …"

"What's going on?" Jennifer asked again.

"You fainted. I carried you to bed."

"I've never fainted." She tucked her legs under her and tried to picture him carrying her to the bedroom, not a terrible thought. "I don't understand why you're here."

He sat opposite, leaning toward her, elbows on his knees. "I couldn't go, not after you fainted." His voice was soft, his eyes sincere. "I was afraid you'd fall and hurt yourself." She was puzzled to see a large suitcase by her front door. Dr. Benson hurried to explain. "We always went away as a family at this time of year," he said, massaging his hands. Jennifer had the urge to reach out and hold them. Elise knocked down a pillow wall and stood up.

"We go to the snow," she said. "But Mommy can't come now." She shot her father a hurt look.

He sighed. "I thought we'd try something new this year, just the two of us." He patted the girl's shoulder. "But I won't leave until I know you're okay," he told Jennifer.

"I'm fine," she said.

"You seem pretty sick," he said with concern. There was gray in his beard. She felt grateful, and a little guilty for her suspicions. She pointed out books she knew Elise would like, pleased when the girl pulled two from the shelf and snuggled back into her pillow cave.

"What do you say, Elise?" Dr. Benson prompted.

"Thank you," Elise said and Jennifer felt the apartment swell with the life it held: a man, a woman, and a child. She lifted the sweat-beaded glass and drank. The orange juice smelled like sunshine. It was cold, sweet on her tongue. It soothed her throat. "Oh," she moaned, eyes closed. "This tastes so good." She licked her lips. When she opened her eyes, he was watching.

He smiled. "Good. Lots of fluids."

Jennifer felt weightless. She laughed, a barking sound, imagining Kelly's face when she told her about Benson. Had Kelly told him she had a crush?

"Do you work with children?" she asked hopefully.

"No. I'm a psychoanalyst. I do couples work." He smiled again.

"I don't know how to thank you," she said, surprised to hear herself offering to cook dinner for him sometime. Her legs chose that moment to wake with a million tiny pinpricks. "Oh!" she cried, straightening them on the table, rubbing them. "Oh, augh." She laughed at his startled expression. "My legs fell asleep," she explained, and felt the creeping return of her shyness. He reached across the table, cupped one of her feet in his hands and began to knead his fingers into the hollows of her sole. He said something about nerves, but she began to giggle and couldn't stop. When she tried to pull her foot away, he held on.

"Ticklish?"

"Yes. No! Stop!" she gasped. He didn't. "Stop it!" she shrieked, and pulled her legs free, wrapped her arms around them and hid her head in her knees. She looked up and her face pulsed with heat.

"Tickling isn't allowed at Happy Trails," Elise announced, poking her head out of the cave.

"What? Why not?" Benson asked. There was an edge to his voice.

"Well … tickling can be uncomfortable and get out of hand."

"Daddy tickles too much," Elise said.

Dr. Benson stiffened. "Don't exaggerate, Elise."

"Sometimes," she whispered with a funny smile.

"I didn't realize you didn't like it," he said. "From now on, no tickling."

Elise agreed with a solemn nod and rebuilt her cushion cave. Dr. Benson watched her for a moment. "Since the divorce, she's been prone to exaggeration, but it's to be expected," he said. Jennifer tried to remember if she'd seen this in Elise at school. He lifted a framed photo from the coffee table in his long-fingered hands.

"Your mother?" He studied the image, her mother's dark eyes and olive skin. Regal, as if the world balanced in the palm of her hand—a photogenic lie. "Are you close?"

Jennifer shook her head. "Close isn't the right word. It's a long story." She wondered what he'd think about the roller coaster of her mother's anxieties and felt certain he'd understand.

"She's beautiful," he said.

"That's how she fools people." Jennifer smoothed her hair, so unlike her mother's dark curls. He returned the photo to the table and sat back, waiting. "It all started with an accident," she told him. "I was five. There was lots of blood. My father said that's what made her so ... nervous." His eyes flicked to the shrouded painting. She thought of the knives, how she hadn't even known she'd painted them. She sank back into the couch.

"May I draw you a bath?" he asked, as if reading her mind.

Tears filled her eyes. Nothing was as it should be.

Jennifer closed her bedroom door and locked the bathroom door behind her. She undressed and slid into her tub with a sigh of pleasure. He'd added bath salts. Eyes closed, she moaned as the heat soaked into her body. She ran her finger along her abdomen and found the puckered pink scar from the accident, a smirk on her belly. When she was a girl, her mother pointed it out at every bath and made her feel ashamed. But she'd only been five—Elise's age—in her Easter hat and yellow dress, running through the Sunday garden party on a bright day, and the knife with its smooth pearl handle glittered beside the cake, so shiny. She'd grabbed it, loving the way the sun scampered down the blade as she ran singing *Three blind mice,* giggling, *see how they run,* chased by adults, a barking dog, and then tripping in slow motion, and falling hard onto the sharp knife and then the screams, the sirened rush, the enormous bed, tubes and beeping machines, and somber, white-coated men, all of it still so vivid in her mind. She rubbed the scar, wondering why her memory was watching, from far away. She slid her fingers over her abdomen, down her thighs and up the insides of her legs. She pictured Dr. Benson's hands cupping her breasts. Three sharp raps sounded on the door.

"What?" she cried, jolting up. Water sloshed out of the bath.

"Are you okay?" Dr. Benson asked.

"I'm fine." She clutched the side of the tub. When she heard him leave, she pulled herself out and dried off. She brushed her teeth and combed her hair, her reflection fogged in the mirror. She pulled on her bathrobe and emerged in a cloud of steam.

Her bed was straightened, the covers turned down. She crawled in, lightheaded. A knock at the door and Dr. Benson came in carrying a tall glass of frothy pink liquid, trailed by Elise.

"What's this?" Jennifer asked, delighted to see him in her apron.

Elise climbed up on the bed. "Strawberry healthy shake," she said through a yawn. Her hair was pulled into a clumsy ponytail.

"Elise," Dr. Benson said. "Get down."

"It's okay." Jennifer patted the comforter. Elise gave her a sleepy smile and curled up beside her. Jennifer wondered how Mrs. Benson could ever have let this go, a sweet life with a darling daughter and a doting husband. Tears stung her eyes at such a loss.

"Daddy put vitamin medicine in to make us better," Elise said.

"Are you sick?" Jennifer asked, concerned.

Dr. Benson handed her the glass. "She's fine. How are you feeling?"

Jennifer sipped the concoction, conscious of his eyes flicking over her breasts, the damp robe clinging to her skin. "Better," she said. The shake was cold, not too sweet, perfect. She set the glass down and leaned into her pillows. "Dr. Benson?"

"Jerry," he insisted.

"Jerry." The sound of his name on her tongue sent a tiny thrill down her arms. "I don't want to spoil your vacation or get either of you sick."

"We're fine," he said.

She grimaced. "I sound like my mother. She's always worried." Her mother had been alarmed to see the queen-sized bed in her apartment. They never went a day without speaking at least twice. Jennifer should call but she resented always having to take care of her mother. She wondered what Dr. Benson would say about that. She pulled her robe closed.

"Drink it all," he said, pointing at the shake. "It will help." He picked a piece of lint off his sweater and roused Elise, who'd fallen sleep. Rubbing her eyes, Elise followed him out and closed the door with a bang that echoed in Jennifer's chest.

★

When she woke again, she felt weighted to her mattress. A long-ago memory surfaced of waking in her crib with her pajama legs pinned together to prevent her from climbing out. She stared at the ceiling and listened to the rasp of her breath, the water tapping at the window, the swish of cars outside. Rain.

When she opened her bedroom door, Dr. Benson was on her sofa. It looked out of place. Had he rearranged the living room furniture? Elise was in her cave with Templeton out of his cage. Jennifer told her to put Templeton back but wasn't sure if she'd said it out loud. Dr. Benson brought a glass of water, he held it while she drank, and led her back to bed. He fluffed her pillows with vigor. She sank into them. He pressed a hand to her forehead and the gesture made her uneasy. When she'd taken the apartment, her mother vacillated erratically between ugly accusations of ingratitude and tearful recitations of the dangers of living alone. To ease her worries, Jennifer agreed to a security system, but she'd lay in bed at night dreading the alarm's shriek, imagining ski-masked men with more than jewels and computers on their minds. She wondered if it still worked. She'd only lived on her own for two years. She loved her apartment and her freedom but had always imagined more friends, maybe parties. No man had ever stayed so long until now, until Dr. Benson.

He gave her the thermometer. She tried to tell him she was fine, but the words came out jumbled. When she pulled the thermometer out, she couldn't read it. He took it from her hand.

"101.3," he said. He shook ibuprofen from a bottle. "Careful." A thick irritation buzzed in her chest. "Drink slowly."

Her hands trembled on the glass. "Dr. Benson." His name was heavy on her tongue.

"Jerry," he said. "Why won't you call me Jerry?" His anger startled her.

"You should go," she said. "I'll be fine."

"I won't leave you here," he said. "Alone." An accusation. He smoothed his trousers with rough jerks of his hands. He'd changed his clothes. How long had he been in her apartment? How long had she slept?

"Where's my clock?" she asked, eyes searching her room.

"Do you want to know the time?" He turned his wrist and pushed up his sleeve.

"I want my clock."

He smiled that smile. "Of course you do." He pointed to the bedside table, crowded with glasses, a tissue box, and a lamp. "There was no room." He pulled the clock from the top drawer of her dresser and plugged it in. Digital 8s flashed at her.

"What time is it?"

"Time to rest." He leaned against her dresser and crossed his arms.

"Where's my phone?" Her voice was sharp.

"Unplugged so you can sleep."

"I should call my mother." The landline was specifically for her mother, who didn't know she had a cell phone. Had Kelly given her cell to Benson?

"Your mother's fine," he said.

"You don't understand."

"Oh," he said, "I think I do."

Jennifer threw off her covers as bile rose up her throat. Benson reached for her.

"Stay," he ordered. "I'll take care of you."

Her stomach lurched. "I'm going to be sick," she moaned and pushed past him into the bathroom. She dropped to her knees and threw up in the toilet.

He patted her back.

"Get out!" she gasped, waving him off.

Elise appeared behind him. "What's the matter?"

Jennifer flushed and sat back against the tub, hollowed out, shivering. Benson hovered in the doorway. Elise looked around him, wide-eyed, holding her nose.

"Miss Jennifer has a hard time needing people," Benson told Elise. "That's why she's alone."

"Get out!" Jennifer shouted hoarsely.

Benson shooed Elise out of the bathroom.

"I meant you," she said. He narrowed one eye; the other was the eye behind the microscope.

"You need medicine. And water. You're dehydrated," he said, and strode out to the kitchen. Jennifer staggered after him and pushed the bedroom door shut. She turned the lock, stumbled back to the bathroom, and held a cool cloth to her face. Her limbs felt leaden. Shaking, she rinsed her mouth. What was wrong with her? In the mirror, she looked startled, her pupils huge.

She sat on her bed.

Benson knocked. "Let me in. You need help."

"I need my phone." She covered her ears to shut out his voice on the other side of the door. Why had she let him stay? A sound came from under her bed. For one frightened second, she imagined him there, until she heard a squeaking sound and the high, quick breathing.

"Come out, honey," she said. A scuffing sound produced Templeton's cage, then Elise dragging the phone by its cord.

Jennifer slid down to the floor and cradled the phone into her lap. "Thank you."

Elise sat beside her. Benson knocked harder. Elise's lower lip trembled. "I like to hide," she whispered.

"I understand." Jennifer wrapped an arm around her, held her close.

"He's very angry now," Elise said.

Benson pounded on the door. Jennifer willed herself to think clearly. *Call 9-1-1.* She lifted the receiver, wondering what she'd say, but there was no dial tone.

Benson paced outside her door—crisp, sharp sounds, back and forth.

A loud squeak made Jennifer jump.

It was the rat on his wheel, frantic, running around and around, eyes bulging, tongue out, panting, running fast.

A Hard Man to Find

Bill told Marlene he had business to take care of, alone. He didn't say he was going after his son.

It rained most of the drive from Oregon up to Seattle on US-101. The frantic twitching of the windshield wipers didn't ease his nerves. He practiced what he'd say to his son, Ryan, but all he could hear were his father's damning words about his inadequacy.

He found his wife's hiding place around midnight, a fourplex shouldered by two pines, on a dark street in a part of town the world had stepped on, hard. He took a small, ugly pleasure at how she'd fallen in the world without him. A Chevy sat in the driveway, another betrayal; she'd sold the Ford, or she had a new man. He wondered which room was Ryan's, watching until the building disappeared behind the cold frosting his windshield.

Bill had coffee in the motel's steamy diner the next morning before sunrise. It was full of people and languages that made him feel foreign. The waitress perched on the edge of his table twirling a pencil rough with teeth marks. She asked if he was new in town, looking him over like he was something special—a nice boost before he went off to confront the woman who'd run away with his son.

Three months earlier, Bill was still in Cleveland at the Last Stallion with the Carjacked—as the guys laid off from the plant called themselves. He'd just worked eleven straight days of bit jobs, still hoping for something permanent, still hoping that his wife, Connie, would bring Ryan home.

The blond cocktail waitress moved through the bar talking and telling stories with a devil smile and pretty eyes. She left happiness in her wake, unlike Connie, who'd become a woman intent on finding fault and measuring other people's misery against her own while never losing count of Bill's drinks.

The Last Stallion wasn't the Carjacked's usual place, but the TV at Riley's was on the fritz that night, a fact he'd later call an omen. He walked to the end of the bar where the waitress placed orders. Her name tag read Marlene and she was curved up just right. She moved like she ran on music, and he imagined that if he put his ear to her belly, he'd hear a melody. She peered up at him with a grin. Lord help him. For Bill, blonds were the gear the world needed to spin. He recalled his father's advice: Don't set your dreams on a beautiful woman, she'll only bring you sorrow. But Bill's sorrow was brunette.

"Where ya sittin', hon?" Marlene's voice was husky like good whiskey is smooth. Her hand on his arm shivered something through him. "I can get you whatever you want."

"Now, that's just what I was thinking." In the mirror behind the bar a big fool grinned back. He straightened, manned up his smile. "A round for the Carjacked." He indicated the men yelling at the widescreen. "And something for yourself, miss."

"A gentleman," she said. A calendar on the wall behind her showed it was August 3rd.

"It's my birthday," he said, stunned. He'd never lost track of the days; he'd always been a Monday-Friday 8-5 man.

Bill's friends howled in outrage over a call against the Indians, who like the Carjacked, were on a losing streak. He dropped into his seat and wondered if Ryan was watching the game. Marlene delivered the drinks.

"On the birthday boy," she said, inspiring hoots and insults. *"May the road rise with you even if your pecker can't, and you don't look a day over sixty."* Bill was thirty-four.

In the seventh inning stretch, some pencilneck at the bar started talking dirt about guys on unemployment tearing America down, which kicked up a shit storm. Bill stayed out of it; he had his eye on Marlene.

At closing time, he waited by the door. The wary bartender eyed him over his limp mustache, but Marlene said, "He seems harmless," and let Bill walk her home.

"You think it's gonna cool off?" Marlene asked, studying the night sky. All the shops were closed, the streets deserted but for the rustle of litter and leaves in the hot breeze.

"Maybe," he said. "But I'm more interested in talking about you."

She gave him a sorrowful smile. "Don't be." She told him her life was a mess, a bad divorce. "Now he's trying to take away my girls."

"I've got a life to put back together myself." He asked where she was from and learned they'd grown up in the same town. He wondered how differently things would have turned out if he'd met her first.

At her apartment, Bill asked to go up. She said no.

"You said yourself I'm a gentleman."

"We'll see." She kissed his cheek and slipped inside.

Walking back to his truck, he felt more hopeful than he had for some time, certain he'd get Ryan back, imagining a second chance. He thought of his older brother, Tommy, who became the engineer his father wanted, lived straightedge for Jesus with a wife he adored; but Tommy's life went balls up and Jesus hadn't granted *him* any second chances.

Bill was twenty-two when he met Connie at a wedding. She was shy and quiet, different from other girls, and taking college classes at the JC. Not usually a drinker, she was wild with champagne love that night. Three months later she was pregnant and wouldn't hear of an abortion, so he married her. His friends warned it was a mistake but she was the first girl to win his father's approval. They had a rushed city hall ceremony, brother Tommy as best man. His father handed Bill a check for fifty dollars and said he hoped Connie could make a man of him.

Bill hadn't thought much about kids, so his love for Ryan bowled him over. From the beginning he vowed to be the father he'd wanted for himself. When he insisted Ryan needed siblings Connie said, "Why? He has you." He and Ryan followed sports, played catch, and fished, always swapping jokes. Ryan would prompt, "Did ya hear the one about ..." and point to Bill to finish. Sometimes they laughed so hard they couldn't breathe.

At first, he convinced himself Connie was good for him, that her lank brown hair and narrow hips were what he wanted. They got along fine while he moved up the line at Ford, but five years in Connie started complaining. For Bill, making people laugh was one of life's great pleasures, but Connie stopped laughing.

Bill's father, a maintenance worker at the mall, had wanted more for his sons, urging them to study medicine or engineering. From the time Bill could walk he could take anything apart and put it back together again, but letters and numbers got squirrelly in his brain. While Tommy became a mechanical engineer, Bill barely graduated high school, one more way he'd let his father down. Connie started siding against Bill when his father came to dinner, itemizing his shortcomings. Bill tried to laugh it off, worried Ryan would think him less of a man.

When Bill lost his job, Connie decreed that ballgames and beer were a luxury they couldn't afford. She never said a word about the odd jobs and double shifts he worked, the home repairs, or the mortgage paid on time. "Beer, jokes, and sports, that's all you are," she'd whine. If it weren't for Ryan, he'd have quit her altogether.

Drinking may have been part of what went wrong but Bill was easier with a shot under his belt and better able to tune out her complaints. He told Connie if Jesus didn't want men to drink, he wouldn't have changed water to wine. A man needed to laugh, raise a little hell sometimes. He'd thought she understood that.

Then one night, after working a grueling twelve hours, Bill opened a beer and she started in dishing up her misery. He told her to get a job. "See how easy it is out there." She screamed, bug-eyed with fury, and Bill saw how much she hated him. She called him a loser in front of Ryan, blaming him for her unhappiness. She wouldn't shut up. When he raised his fist, the fear in her eyes rattled him. He turned his anger to the wall, looking for her pinched face in the plaster, and the sheetrock flew. Ryan shrieked, "Stop!" He looked at Bill like he was a monster, then bolted for his room and locked the door.

Bill sat in his truck, massaging his sore hand, waiting for Ryan after school the next day. He tooted his horn and Ryan waved, his smile half grimace.

"Hop in." Bill pointed to him. "You scream—"

"—I scream," Ryan said dully.

In the truck eating ice cream, Bill apologized for his temper. "I'm trying hard to take care of us, but your mom won't give me a break."

Ryan thought about this. "Were you gonna punch her?

"A man doesn't hit a woman."

Ryan circled his ice cream with his tongue.

"But I wanted to."

They drove home in silence. As Bill turned into the driveway, Ryan said, "Knock-knock," but the joke fell away, unfinished. Bill roughed his son's hair and invited him on his weekend fishing trip with the Carjacked, though he'd have to miss school on Monday. Ryan grinned, his chin pink with strawberry ice cream.

Connie said no. "There's only two weeks until summer and he's failing math." A counselor had recently labeled Ryan with an alphabet soup of troubles that just proved school sucked for boys. Bill learned about dyslexia then, how symbols got confused in some people's brains. The only name his father had for it was stupid. Bill felt bad Ryan inherited this from him, yet pleased his son was more like him than Connie. In the end, Bill went fishing without Ryan, promising a backpacking trip when school got out. He returned the following Monday night to an empty house and a note: *We're leaving. You're a violent man and we don't feel safe.*

Ryan's school Principal twisted her hands, explaining that Connie took Ryan's records and left no forwarding address. Bill checked his bank account; his only surprise was that she hadn't taken it all. At the police station he learned that Connie had filed a complaint against him. Bill told a cop they'd had a fight and yeah, he'd punched a wall, but never touched her. "She took my son!" The cop just said, "Give her time. They always come back, if just for money."

Bill roamed the town, even went to the church Connie dragged Ryan to on Sundays, but no one had seen her. It was weeks before he cornered his father-in-law, a small, nervous man whose wife had run out on him too. All he'd say was, "She moved west."

He should have pushed the cops harder. He'd have gone looking himself, but where? He drank instead, nursing his anger over how he'd been wronged, and missing Ryan.

A week after meeting Marlene, Bill took her to a Chinese restaurant before her shift at the Last Stallion. He told her about Connie and Ryan; she told Bill about her divorce.

"Irreconcilable differences—he's an asshole and I'm not." She had a way of putting things that made Bill laugh. "I'm living in a donut's hole without the sugar." Bill asked if she still loved him. "Absotively not! He's already got someone new."

"The man's a fool to give you up."

"You still love yours?"

"Not sure I ever did," he said, knowing it was true.

Marlene had wanted to go west, too, to be near her sister, but her ex wouldn't leave his mother. She wanted her girls to grow up with family, "in the redwoods, by the blue Pacific—a place to be alive." Bill liked the sound of that. Marlene's plan was to go to her sister's, get settled with a job, then send for her girls, who were six and eight and blond like Marlene. He met the girls over pizza one night. Marlene introduced Bill as her "friend" who had "a son named Ryan." She cooed over her daughters' crayon drawings, enjoying them in a way Connie hadn't enjoyed Ryan. She reminded Bill of his mother, a loving woman, soft and tender who was never loved properly in return. They toasted Big Fred with Shirley Temples. That was Marlene's name for God and a secret they kept from her ex. "Big Fred and I are on a first name basis," she said, "after all the hell he's put me through."

"Where's Ryan?" the girls asked, swiveling their heads; for half-a-second Bill scanned the pizza parlor, too. Marlene said, "Ryan's on a trip with his mother," but the girls' questioning little faces shamed Bill for letting the months slide by, hoping the cops were right and Connie would bring Ryan home.

At his house the next day, there was a message on the machine. "Dad?" A breath. "Dad? You there? It's me. Ryan." Bill played the message over and over, frantic for a number to call back. He repaired his busted wall and filed a missing person's report. After a sleepless night, he hired a lawyer to sue for desertion; it was going to take time and money he didn't have, but the phone call told Bill that Ryan wanted to be found. He changed his outgoing message: *Ryan. I'm looking for you. Call my cell*, reciting the number just in case. Bill's plan was: Help Marlene move west and find Ryan.

★

The day they left, he put his toolbox, three suitcases, and an ice chest in the back of his truck, glad that Marlene didn't have much baggage. He took her to say goodbye to her girls on the way out of town. She squeezed them close while the mother-in-law chewed her thumbnail, keeping a wary eye. Marlene told her babies she loved them and was going to find a sweet place for them all to live. She blew kisses from the truck. The youngest cried, "Mommy," reaching out her chubby little arms, but Grandma grabbed her hand and pulled her inside. Once Bill's truck rounded the corner, Marlene slumped in the seat, hands to her chest.

"Can you hear my heart?" she moaned. "Ripping in two?"

He rolled down the window and sucked in air to keep his wits.

"It's a terrible thing," he said, but told himself to let her cry, that what was needed was distance. He floored it to the interstate, his compass set west to the redwoods and Marlene's sister, who lived in a big house by a river in a green place where they were welcome.

Bill left Cleveland taking I-90 to I-80 past the plant; he tipped an imaginary hat, then gave Ford the finger. He'd worked hard, moved up the ranks to foreman, made himself a man he'd like to know. He'd taken Ryan to work a few times to show him off, reveling in his son's pride.

"I know what you're thinking," Marlene said.

"Okay, Crystal Ball Woman," Bill said. "Reveal my mind."

"You're probably asking yourself, 'What the hell am I doing with a failure, a woman who runs out on her kids?'" She got teary again.

How could he judge her when he'd lost his own son? He asked if she planned on crying the whole trip. "If so," he said, "I'll have to pick up a sump pump." She twirled a strand of her blond hair, looking out from behind her sunglasses like she was trying to decide. She wiped her eyes and used her tissue to clean off the dashboard.

"No use wasting good tears," she said, and dusted the cab. "Sorrow," she said, "is my new cleaning agent!"

He pulled her close to give her some love. Even with her troubles she could laugh, and that was medicine he needed in his life. In Defiance, they made a pit stop. Bill bought plastic cups and made gin rickeys from the ice chest to lift them up.

They made it to Fort Wayne before five, the sun hard in their faces. He wanted to check on his brother, who'd been after him to visit. On the exit ramp he noticed the front right tire was riding low but was relieved it was just a nail and could be patched.

Marlene said, "That's Big Fred's way of telling us we're on the right path."

At a service station, he called Tommy, but the secretary at his office said he no longer worked there. He tried to remember the last time they'd talked. Tommy answered his home phone and told Bill to hurry.

They arrived with pizza and a six-pack of coke; Tommy didn't drink, for Jesus. Bill warned Marlene not to mention Big Fred but when they stepped onto Tommy's porch, they found Jesus stuffed in boxes: pictures, crosses, and books. Dust and water stains said he'd been there a while.

Tommy opened the door and threw his arms around Bill who was surprised to see his big brother so stooped and gray at thirty-eight. He told Bill he'd given up on God, "after he couldn't be bothered to send one little miracle to save my sweet wife who did so much for his son." Bill didn't do business with God; knowing sin was invented to make a man feel ashamed and he already had his father and wife for that.

Tommy and his wife, Joanne, shared a sweet love. Bill brought Connie along, once. She'd disapproved, no doubt hating their happiness. Joanne, a round, kind woman, unable to have children of her own, had doted on Ryan.

Tommy grabbed a handle of whiskey off the counter, faced Bill across the sticky oak table and poured. The house was a mess and smelled sour, like an old man, like things gone bad.

"Haven't you got a hello for Marlene?" Bill pulled her onto his lap. Tommy slapped a hand to his head.

"I'm losing my manners without my Joanne. And now Dad's gone too." Tommy shook his sorrowful head, poured Marlene a drink and asked, "Where's our Ryan?"

"Connie ran off and took him. I'm tracking them down."

Tommy looked at him hard. "Connie's one miserable bitch." But those were the last words Bill could agree with as his brother kept talking. Crazy talking. Marlene raised her eyebrows.

"Now Tommy," Bill said to his brother's conspiracy theories about ISIS, the EPA giving Joanne her disease, and Planned Parenthood murdering babies. "What the hell are you talking about?" Tommy was never a nut job beyond being a holy roller. "Where're you getting your information? University of Jimmy Beam?" Bill suggested he read a book and reminded him he'd been better off with the Holy one. "It's terrible you lost Joanne, but people die, it's just … the way of things."

Tommy gave him a wild look, hopped up, leaned forward, eyes sparking. He lifted his side of the table, like he was weighing it, like he might flip it over.

"I didn't mean anything. Calm down," Bill yelled.

"Hey now," Marlene said. She opened a window above a sink with dirty dishes to let in a frail breeze. She gave Bill a look that said what he could see himself. "Tommy, honey?" she said. "Tell me a story about your Joanne. I'm real sorry I never met her."

Tommy exhaled a long, whistled breath and collapsed in his chair. Marlene served up the pizza, gone cold, as

Tommy bragged of Joanne's fishing prowess. Bill, no longer hungry, passed his slices to Tommy who looked like he hadn't eaten in weeks. Marlene smiled, listening to him ramble. Bill was just happy he'd climbed down off his crazy horse. It was unnerving seeing Tommy, caved in with grief, defeated, the one who'd done everything right. He took Marlene's hand under the table and traded a squeeze, thankful she was there. Thankful she wasn't Connie.

When they went to bed, Marlene and Bill started moving together, taking their comfort in each other until Tommy banged on the wall and said, "Mercy. Have some mercy," which took the fun out of it altogether.

In the darkest hour of the night Bill was taking a leak when Marlene screamed. He raced back to find Tommy standing over her, dazed, ghost-like. He steered Tommy back to bed and sat with him until he was sure his brother was asleep, watching as Tommy snored. Moonlight through the window lit his cadaverous face. His open mouth, missing two back teeth, gave off a sour stink. Who would love him now? Bill was sixteen when his mother died, and he lost the one person who'd truly loved him. Trucks moaned and rattled on the interstate half-a-mile away. Bill wondered where so many people were going in the middle of the night and why folks couldn't just stay put and love each other.

They packed up before the sun, and left Tommy a note of thanks for the hospitality. Bill wanted to say something to cheer him, but what can words do for a man who's given up? Marlene slept on the seat as he drove. He was an asshole for not visiting his brother more after he'd lost the love of his life. The sunset sky bled colors like it was reflecting all the hurt in the world and it was hard not to let it get a hold on him. He rode for miles alongside a vintage red Impala, a Devil's Tower sticker on its bumper. A woman sat close under the driver's arm; two kids slept in back. The man waved, his smile so certain of happiness that Bill had a furious urge to wrench his wheel and bump him off the road.

Oregon was pretty, but the low-hanging clouds and the closeness of the evergeens felt claustrophobic after the big skies of the open road. They got to Marlene's sister's place late the next night. Jan was blond, too, with a cute wrinkly-nosed smile. Thinner and more intense than Marlene, she looked out from behind her glasses like she had you figured out. Her husband, Richard, was a tall, frail man, though in pictures on the wall he was big and strong. He'd just won a cancer marathon, limping to the finish line.

"I'm stronger every day," he said, but the weakness of his voice terrified Bill.

"I've got my tools." Bill jerked his thumb to his truck. "I like to keep busy. Let me know if you need anything done."

The next night, they sat around the dinner table with Jan's and Richard's kids, drinking wine while Marlene and

Jan shared funny childhood stories, the kids egging them on. Richard talked up Bill's fixing things he hadn't been able to get to "since the bad Mr. C came to town." He rubbed his fuzzy head and made cancer jokes. Everyone laughed. It was how a family should be. The boy, Aiden, was a baseball fanatic, an encyclopedia of stats, like Ryan. Later, Bill tossed the ball with him, waking the ache for his son he'd been trying to hide down deep.

When the kids went to bed, Marlene told Jan the wrecking-ball story of her divorce, how she'd temporarily lost custody. Jan paced from fridge to sink.

"I can't believe you left the state. You'll never get them back now."

Richard tried to shut Jan up, but she was steaming.

"Don't you know, Richard?" Marlene said. "Jan's always right."

Aiden, wide-eyed in the doorway, asked what was wrong. Richard hustled him back to bed, assuring him everything would be okay. Bill hoped he was right.

Jan asked why Marlene didn't call for help. "We could have found you a better lawyer."

Bill saw that Jan was the sister who did everything right, went to college, and though younger by two years, seemed certain and solid in ways that Marlene was soft. Jan was an engineer with Boeing, like Richard. They made good money and had insurance, so even a thing like cancer couldn't bring them to their knees.

In bed, Bill told Marlene he believed in their starting-over plan, but Marlene curled, cheek to knees, like a little girl. She said if this was starting over it wasn't much fun. It gave him a hollow feeling. He'd been leaning on her optimism.

They stayed clear of the house during the day until Jan cooled off and Marlene was herself again. Bill found construction work, and Marlene got a job at a Hallmark and took every shift they'd give her. She called her girls each night. Eventually, the sisters made up. Marlene agreed that Jan was right and accepted her offer to hire her a lawyer.

Two weeks later, Bill parked in front of Jan and Richard's house after work. He popped a beer and sat watching the windows filled with light bought with the kind of money that kept trouble at bay. With Richard's help and Bill's experience, he'd landed a solid job at the United Streetcar plant in Clackamas, earning the best money he'd ever made. Bill's father always said a man made his own luck. Bill wanted to believe it. He told himself he was only thirty-four, and maybe there was still time. He'd been carrying Ryan's picture in his pocket, memorizing every bit of his face, but what good was that doing? He pulled out his phone and called Connie's father, counting the rings. Since leaving Ohio, he'd tried the man five times. This time he answered.

"A son needs his father," Bill said, startled by his own loud voice. His lie, that the FBI was on Connie's trail, inspired the man to cough up an address. Seattle, only one-hundred-seventy miles away.

Bill sat for a long time listening to the river tumble and sigh.

The morning was dark in Seattle. Rain blurred the windshield as Bill drove. He felt underwater and thought of geese—or turkeys?—who drowned because they hadn't the sense to stop looking up, openmouthed, at the rain. He parked across the street from Connie's, screwing up his nerve. The shabby brown fourplex resembled her mood; nothing for a garden but flattened weeds.

"Look out," he said to no one. "Here I come." He rehearsed his practiced speech but stayed put. Until Jan's voice echoed in his head, asking Marlene what her little girls must think. He shoved his door open, stepped into the soggy world, pulled his jacket over his head, ran to the door, and pushed the doorbell. He didn't hear it chime. He knocked.

The door swung wide. A shirtless kid in pajama bottoms squinted up at him. Ryan. His dark hair stood up on one side. His eyes went wide with recognition. He grinned, then frowned, putting up his guard, making Bill proud to see his son knew a thing or two.

"Hey." Bill longed to clap his arms around him. "You are a hard man to find." He smiled, his cheeks twitching with nerves. Ryan's brow creased with suspicion, confirming Bill's guess that Connie had fed him lies.

"Can I come in?"

Ryan checked over his shoulder, then pointed to the street. "I'll come out," he whispered.

The door closed softly. Bill wondered if Connie was home and who else was there. He ran back to his truck, brushed off the seat, and stuffed receipts and tissues in the glove compartment. He turned on his radio, then turned it off. Ryan had grown in five months. He had a new life. Bill wondered if schools were better in Seattle. Connie always gave Bill her blaming face when Ryan struggled with math. That face in his head stirred up a panic, fear that Ryan wouldn't come out, imagining the terrible lies Connie had told him. When the front door opened, Bill was surprised to find his engine running, the truck in gear, his foot on the brake. He turned it off. Ryan sauntered down the path barefoot, in jeans and his Indians hoodie, oblivious to the cold. He climbed into the cab.

"Hey." He sat, rigid, hand on the door, waiting for Bill to begin.

"I've been looking for you. You okay?"

Ryan nodded, gave him an uncertain sidelong glance.

"I've missed you," Bill said wondering what rules his father would have for a moment like this, but his father would never have been in such a spot.

"How are you?" Ryan asked, color rising in his face.

"Good. Now that I've found you."

Ryan's feet tapped a nervous beat.

"So," Bill said. "Did you hear the one about—" He clutched the steering wheel, wondering how a man who could fix anything had no clue how to seal them back together.

Ryan, eyebrows raised, waited for Bill to reveal the humor in their story, how they'd ended up this way in the world, so far apart. The doubt in his face made Bill afraid that he'd already failed at being the father he'd wanted, that it might be too late.

"Dad?" Ryan bounced his knees, fast and nervous, shivering the truck. Rain pounded the cab's metal roof.

Bill tried to laugh but coughed, a strangled sound. "So, this guy goes fishing, catches one this big—" He inched his palms wide, then wider, a joke they'd shared many times. "Huge. He brings it home to show his son, but he'd—" Bill snapped his fingers — "disappeared."

"Mom said you'd come." Ryan's voice cracked. "Why didn't you?"

"Hard to find someone if you don't know where they are, if they run 2500 miles away."

Ryan blinked rapidly, trying not to cry.

"When I didn't show, what'd she tell you?" Bill set a hand on Ryan's knees to still them.

"That you probably changed your mind."

"Jesus," Bill said, fighting down his fury. "You didn't believe that, did you? When I got home, you were gone. Cops said you'd come back. I waited 'cuz I had no idea where you were."

Ryan looked stricken. "I called you."

"Yeah. But I didn't know how to call you back."

Ryan inhaled sharply and collapsed back against his seat. They sat listening to the raindrops, the cab steaming up.

"How'd you find me?" Ryan asked finally, his voice shaky.

When he was a child, Bill's mother read him a story of a bunny who runs away, and his mother always finds him. Bill read the story to Ryan many times, making the hero a father rabbit. His father never read to him, and it wasn't until he died that Bill learned he'd flunked out of high school. Suddenly he understood: his father was dyslexic.

"Jesus!"

Ryan jumped. "What?"

Bill shook his head. "Listen, Ryan, I'd never stop looking for you."

"Okay, but how'd you find me?"

Bill swallowed. "FBI helped."

Ryan turned to face him, eager for the story and scooted forward on his seat, his face tense. He made a fist and rapped his knuckles against the dashboard—*knock-knock.*

Bill watched the world disappear beyond the fogged glass of the cab, searching his mind for a joke to make things right, but in that moment, nothing was funny. Instead, he began to tell his son the story of his own life, about trying to do his best, hoping to tell it simple and true, hoping it might be enough.

A Whole Hand

Brenna turns the ashtray over to see "Sean" carved in crooked letters, fourteen years ago, when he turned five, "A whole hand!" The lumpy gift in her palm, a treasure, reminds her of the chubby little fingers she'd held in hers, the hand that brought surprises. "Pick, Mommy," he'd say, grinning, arms tucked behind his back as he peered through the gold-rimmed glasses he'd worn to train his lazy eye. She'd tap one of his arms, aiming for the wrong one to feed his excitement. "No! Pick again!" His giggle was all glittering water over colorful stones as he offered her a gift in his dirty palm: a crushed flower, a seedpod, a dead bug.

She hasn't heard from him in over two weeks.

Outside, beyond the lace curtains, Wyatt, her older son, home for Thanksgiving, works on his truck. He resents her insistence that he spend this Thanksgiving break at home instead of joining a college friend's annual hunting trip in the mountains. But she wants him close, away from guns. His broad shoulders and attention are turned to the porch, where Brenna's father-in-law, Buck, calls orders.

Her sons' only living grandparent, Buck, moved in three years ago and took command. Her husband acquiesced as he always did with his father. Wind snaps the flag and rattles the windows. She shivers. Her fingers make the sign of the cross, a lifelong habit, fraught now.

A tang of sulfur tickles her nose as she strikes a match, lights a cigarette, sucks hard, trying to suffocate the panic that rises when she thinks of Sean, so far away. At nine, he begged her to quit smoking and his hazel eyes, wide with worry, convinced her. She took it up again the day he shipped out, and now the dish in the shape of his small hand is her smoking companion.

Her reflection in the window reminds her she is letting herself go. A white center stripe divides her brown hair; she's grown so thin her cheeks looked etched on her face. She sits with her coffee in her wooden chair at the kitchen table, mistress of this one room where his picture, dimpled grin and long dark curls, hangs on the wall. Beside it is a photo of him in his uniform with his grandfather. It was Buck who pushed him to enlist.

She moves the ashtray on the gingham grid of the tablecloth like a chess piece and smokes while she waits, as she waits every afternoon, for the mail truck to turn down her drive. Sean knows she loves letters, his voice made tangible in his handwriting. "Snail mail," he calls it, amused by her old-fashioned preference but he writes when he can.

Last night a news report: a bombing, three Americans killed. Her fingers on the remote raced through the TV stations, searching to not find him, but the casualties of war are forgotten now in America's daily news. While she flipped through channels, her husband worked on the kitchen sink's drain. He won't look at the TV or papers. And whenever she rushes down the street to use her cousin's computer to search the Corps website, to see which company was hit, he tells her she's torturing herself with useless worry. At first it infuriated her and she called him callous. Now she's relieved not to share her angst. Once, they were everything to each other and happy.

The first time her father-in-law tried to comfort her, saying, "Don't worry. Sean's having the adventure of a lifetime; it'll make a man of him," she'd had to fight to keep her hands from slapping his face. All she said was, "Don't." Her now deceased mother-in-law had told her of Buck's Vietnam hangover—the nightmares, the sweats and shaking—how for years he jumped at every noise. Now he glorifies his service. Did he train his mind to offer only carefully cropped memories?

There was no dancing in the streets to welcome Sean's company, no wide-open arms or gratitude as the President promised. She imagines Sean there, innocent and earnest in the dust and sandstorms, burka-clad mothers and displaced men eyeing him with mistrust, hatred. She shakes her head and reminds herself they are powerless, too.

When her husband isn't working at the plant, he labors on the house, his own balm for the agony of wait and worry. He reroofed the garage since the last letter came, and in the past few days, while they had no email, no letter, he helped Wyatt rebuild his Chevy's engine.

Wyatt listened to her instead of the men and applied to college. Her husband argued, "Enlist in ROTC, go for free." But Brenna knows ROTC means the opposite of free and insisted on paying with the tiny nest egg of her inheritance. Wyatt's a senior, killing himself studying engineering and computer science, all A's to prove his worth absent the Semper Fi bona fide. He tries so hard to please his elders, these men, both ex-Marines, who can't understand putting college before country. She sees the mantle of their disappointment in the set of her son's shoulders.

"Mom. You should get a computer," Wyatt said when she'd returned that morning from checking email at the library. "Join the modern era." She reminded her son that she had a part-time job at the library with a computer all set up for her there. He gave her the look his Grandpa Buck bestows on idiots. But she doesn't want a computer at home. Buck has never used one, and she doesn't want him starting now, doesn't want him taking over her watch. Besides, it's quieter in the library, and she's working on her Associate degree and seeing what's possible.

She rereads Sean's last letter, seventeen days old, saved with the others. *Hi Mom, I'm okay, just hot as hell and bored. Thanks for the books, socks, and stuff. The guys loved the brownies. Please don't worry, Love, Sean.*

She pours lemonade, carries it out to Wyatt, and leans against his truck. He takes the glass in his large hands and thanks her. She doesn't see the woman passing the gate in time to avoid her. Sean's high school English teacher.

Brenna heard she was a liberal who stirred up trouble about the wars. Not enough. The woman calls hello, a backpack slung over one shoulder, her black curls wild around her face. She asks about Sean.

"He's fine, thank you," Brenna says, revealing nothing, but pleased that at least one person remembers the country is still at war.

"He was such a special boy." The woman turns her sharp eyes on Wyatt. When her questions reveal he's in college, she brightens. "Good for you. That's the smart decision." She shakes her head. "We lost too many local boys to this war."

Wyatt shoves his hands into his pockets, stares at a passing car.

"Sean is still a special boy, and you—" Brenna jabs her finger at the woman.

"Mom!" Wyatt says under his breath. "Be cool."

She rushes back inside, leaving the teacher open-mouthed. Wyatt follows her to the kitchen.

"Mom?" His worried expression reminds her of his little-boy face before he cried.

"I'm sorry, Wyatt. I'm just so sick of people saying …"

"I know," he says. "Me too."

She wonders what stupid things they say at his college, people who have to stamp his brother's life with judgments or inane commendations.

Wyatt raises his empty glass. "Thanks for this." He sets it in the sink, then surprises her with a kiss on the cheek.

"You are a fine and noble man," she tells him, furious that anyone would make him feel otherwise but he's already out the door.

The cat jumps into Brenna's lap as soon as she sits. She rubs the cat's silky fur, the only other female in the house. Brenna grew up in this old farmhouse with four sisters, scattered now—west and north—her parents gone.

Buck works his chair back and forth on the porch, *creak—thump, creak—thump*, as he drinks the afternoon coffee she makes for him in his Greatest Grandpa mug. Does he believe that playing sentry will keep bad news from turning down the drive? Or is he waiting for the government car with its two officers?

She resents his vigil. He has no right. He's the one who pointed Sean to the few, the proud, while she'd secretly scribbled letters of protest to the White House and a President she once trusted. Her husband only said, "It's the boy's decision. Let it be."

She watches her husband outside, leaning into the wind, pushing the mower, his hair cropped short, his face determined as the leaves rain yellow and red. He's wearing sandals, and she shudders at an onslaught of images of blood and severed toes. Once, she'd loved him to distraction, so handsome in his uniform, believing they were of one mind, imagining a future wrapped around the family they'd make together, a future she'd had no age-earned wisdom to foresee. Now she sees a man surrendered, a stranger to the husband she invented, subject to a father he allows to rule his roost.

"Mail's here," Buck shouts. No need. She's heard the truck gears shifting, the crunch of gravel on her drive. Brenna pulls one final drag into her lungs, deep and damaging, snuffs her cigarette out in her coffee cup. Clutching the lumpy ashtray, his whole hand in hers, she hurries out to meet it.

Magic Fingers

Mama was tired of everything broken. She stormed into the diner from the utility room, where the Roadside Motel bent in the corner like an L. She grabbed the wall phone, dialed Phil's Electric, and leaned against the counter; a hand jammed into the pocket of her tight jeans. She told Phil she was done jerry-rigging the water heater and asked real sweet when the parts would be in. Her hair was stuffed into her Lone Star cap; grease streaked her left cheek.

"I can't wait that long," she said. "Hot showers and cold beer are the only reason people stop here." She listened, chewing her lip, then hung up in disgust.

Chuck stood, tucked in his Dr. Pepper shirt, and offered to have a look, but Mama never let the customers "fix" things because they'd think she owed them something and they usually just made things worse.

"When's he coming?" I asked.

"Who?" Her eyes went sparky.

"Phil. What'd he say?"

She mimicked Phil's deep voice. "'Hell no, Rosie, they come for your chili.'"

Just then, the lady in #3 waddled in wearing a bath towel. On a woman her size it didn't cover much. She was red all over and said all hot and nasty, "Who's in charge?"

Mama raised her hand like a schoolgirl. "Unfortunately, that'd be me."

"What kinda fleabag motel you runnin' here?" The woman glared at the fly strip in the window. "No hot water last night. None this morning."

"I'm sorry," Mama said. "The boiler blew. I'm waiting on parts."

The men hunched at the counter stopped arguing about the Rangers to peek over their shoulders. They were always there, like part of the furniture, talking, drinking coffee, telling jokes, and teasing Mama. Always teasing.

"Put your fuckin' teeth back in," the woman said. Sheriff Tom stood, showed off his badge, his hair combed careful to make the most of it. He offered to wash out her mouth. "Kiss my ass," she said and stomped out.

One of the men hooted and the other men's shoulders started to shake. Most were drivers stopping regular for an hour or a night. Their backs advertised what they drove; today it was UPS brown, Chuck's Dr. Pepper red, and Mike wearing America's colors for Chevy. Sheriff Tom always sat at the table by the window where the eyelet curtains covered him in snowflakes of light. He spread out his papers like it was his office. Mama threatened to charge the county rent, but she never would because he was like family.

"Make yourself useful, Tom," she said. "Arrest that woman."

"Didn't look like she was packing a weapon."

"Other than a razor tongue," Chuck said, setting them off again. Mama fought a smile, but her frown won out. I would have played the jukebox to cheer her up but it was on the fritz, too.

"You're in a mood," Tom said. Mama sat down at his table and talked about moving to California, a sure sign her temper was up. For weeks, I'd found her on the porch frowning down our highway like something terrible was headed our way.

I went out on the porch with Noah, the white dog my daddy gave me six years ago on my third birthday, just before he ran off. The new interstate to the north had drawn traffic off our highway, and business got slower every year. Mama got the Roadside from her daddy. I thought of it as a family heirloom, but she said, "No, more like a curse." She wanted to sell and live by the sea, but the For Sale sign she put up the year I started third grade hadn't raised any interest.

A flatbed—Magruder's Music and Motion—turned off the highway. He came once a month to service the Magic Fingers boxes on the motel beds, the coffee shop jukebox, and the pinball machines. Our life was so regular we knew what day it was by who drove in off the 41, but lately he'd been showing up at least once a week. I called Mr. Magruder the Magic Fingers Man, but never to his face. It was a funny name for a man who looked so serious, big and tall with black-rimmed glasses and brown hair cut short and bristly, like his mustache. He always wore tan slacks and a short-sleeved white shirt; he looked the same all the time, neat and quiet. All the drivers called Mama Rosie, but he called her by her real name, Esther, or he just called her Ma'am. He came up our driveway, just a scratched-out track in the dirt, whipping up a dust cloud that looked like he was being erased.

Today, he surprised me in new sunglasses and a blue shirt with a tie. When I tried to picture my daddy, I saw the Magic Fingers Man. There were always men around the Roadside, but he was different; didn't pat you on the head, ask your grade or if you had a boyfriend. He was comfortable.

"Mr. Magruder," I said when he reached the steps. "You're nice like pajamas." He flipped up his sunglasses, gave me his sweet smile and sat down beside me.

"How's that, Miss McKane?" I loved his 'bama accent. Noah nosed between us, thumping his tail.

"She means she likes you," Mama said from the door. I didn't know she was there. His face lit up and gave me a new view of his looks. He hopped up to light Mama's cigarette. I made a face at her. She'd promised to quit.

"You ever think of growing out your hair?" I asked him. "You could be a looker."

Mama coughed. "Jessie McKane!" But he laughed and said something that made Mama laugh, too. She always told me, "Marry a man who makes you laugh, doll. Life is hard, you need someone to help you hunt down the humor in it." But she was frowning down the road again.

He followed her gaze. "Everything alright?"

"Could be worse. And you?"

"Fine, now that I'm with two beautiful girls."

"We didn't expect you back so soon." Mama was twenty-seven and so pretty when she smiled.

"I got your message about the jukebox," he said.

I followed them inside.

"Magruder," Sheriff Tom said. "Looking sharp." Whistles sounded off from the counter. "Hot date?" He winked at me, knowing I hoped Mr. Magruder could be something more.

Mr. Magruder set his toolbox by the Superman pinball. "My date's with a jukebox that won't play Esther the music she deserves." He gave Mama a love look. I hurried to make his coffee the way he liked it, white and sweet.

I finished my chores and followed him out to the rooms to help. We had eleven at the Roadside, all the same, except the dresser and bed flip-flopped with the bath from room to room.

"You must be real smart to invent that machine," I said as we rolled up his quarters. Sometimes I pushed my foot against the wall, to rock my own bed when it was too hot to sleep. "If I'd thought it up, Mama wouldn't have to work so hard."

He laughed. "A guy named Houghtaling invented it. Sold a million. He worked in a motel like you and your mama. At first, he made the staff lay under the bed. When a customer flicked a switch, they had to shake the mattress back and forth."

I tried to imagine this, then saw his smile.

"You're teasing." I slapped his arm. "But how'd you get it?"

His gaze drifted far away, out the window. "A girl named Lorene." He chuckled.

We were going into #5 when I heard Arlene, our mail carrier, singing her Patsy Cline. She sang so loud Mama said they could hear her in the next county. I ran to the porch as she drove up waving a letter from Carla in her meaty hand. Carla was my best friend who'd just moved to South Carolina.

Noah put his paws on her car door, begging for a biscuit. Arlene gave him one and he plopped down in the driveway to eat it. "Dogs are like men," she always said. "You have to soothe their savage with sweet." Arlene nodded at the flatbed. "I see your man's in town."

"He's wearing a tie," I said. Arlene raised her painted-on eyebrows.

Mama came out to get the mail. Arlene didn't get out of her car on account of her knees. She put Mama in a good mood with her secrets and jokes she said were too "risky" for my ears.

"Mama?" I asked. "Don't you want to clean up a little?"

"Look who's talkin'. Show me your feet." The bottoms were black. "Exactly!" she said.

I put my letter in my pocket and sat in my swing in the big laurel tree. Mama looked over at me while she talked to Arlene. When they finished, Arlene tooted her horn and drove off, her car leaning hard to the driver's side until it was swallowed up in heat lines off the highway.

A big rig passed her coming fast. Its boxcars sounded empty by the way they rattled and clacked. The truck whooshed, slowing down, and the brakes growled.

I hollered, "Noah, git!" but he just looked at me and smiled. I raced to grab his collar and drag him out of the way, terrible pictures flashing through my mind. The big rig pulled in just beyond the diner, stirring up dust so bad it got in my teeth. I didn't know the rig. My heart pounded. What if I hadn't been outside? When the dust settled, I squatted to see underneath. Cowboy boots hit the ground on the other side and the man shined them up quick on the back of his jeans.

"Hey!" I yelled, ready to give him heck for nearly killing my dog but he beat me into the diner. "C'mon Noah."

Inside, Tom was frowning at the man, shaking his head. "If it isn't Wes McKane."

My daddy's name! Wes sat on the counter, something Mama didn't allow, and offered a wager on the new Texas Rangers. The counter men always came to life over baseball.

"Keep an eye on your wallets," Tom said.

"Where is she?" Wes asked.

He wasn't like I remembered.

"Guess you're not here to pay me my money," Tom said. I stepped closer, nervous, about to say I was right there, but Tom said, "She's out back. With Magruder," and got himself more coffee. "The water heater blew. She keeps tinkering with it." He gave Wes a mean smile. "But she's always had a blind eye for lost causes." That's when Mama came in.

"I sure hope everybody likes cold showers, because—" I don't know what I expected, but not the scowl she put on.

"I was just wondering what a man's got to do to get service around here," Wes said.

She stepped behind the counter, looked him up and down. "Depends on the man."

Wes smiled. "Beautiful as ever. Isn't she, boys?" They agreed, nodding their heads. She put a hand to her hair, still tucked in her cap. At least she'd wiped off the grease. "No wonder these men hang round," Wes said, and punched the red logo on Chuck's sleeve.

"Nah," Chuck said. "We come for her chili."

Mama's laugh made everything easier. Wes looked skinnier than in the one picture I had of him, but he still had that big smile. His hair was brown like mine. And the Magic Fingers Man's. Wes offered to buy a round but got no takers.

"You have engine trouble?" Tom asked him. Mama shot him a warning look. "Well, some of us have been waiting on him." Tom jerked his head toward me and went back to his paperwork, muttering, his mouth pulled down like he tasted something bad.

UPS stood, tucked in his brown shirt, and made a finger gun at Tom. "Bye Rosie," he said. "See ya, Jess." The screen door banged shut.

Wes spun around, eyes wide as his smile. He had dimples like me. "Look at you!" Everyone did.

"Hi," was all I could say. I slipped behind the counter next to Mama.

"Let's get you a Pepsi," Wes said. "We're celebrating!"

"I like Dr. Pepper."

"That's my girl," Chuck said, puffing up.

Mama opened a Pepper, eyes on Wes.

"I'm Jessie," I told him.

"Yes, you are! Named for my mother."

"Really?"

"You got so big." Wes shook his head. "And blue-eyed pretty like your mama."

I couldn't help grinning. "I'm ten next week." I stood tall as I could.

"What do you want?" Mama asked.

"I said in my letter I was coming home."

"You wrote us?" I never saw any letter.

"Sure, I wrote," Wes said. "Lots of times." Mama wouldn't look me in the eye.

Chuck drummed his hands on the counter and stood, said something about a thirsty world. Chevy Mike drained his coffee and followed him out.

"Wanna see Noah?" I asked Wes.

"Is he another man your mama's keeping around here?"

"No! He's our dog. Remember? I took good care of him just like you said." Mama made a noise. Wes stood, straightened his big silver belt buckle, and followed me out to Noah's shady spot on the porch.

"Hey, buddy," he said. I wanted to ask Wes where he'd been, but my throat went tight. He lit a cigarette and peered inside the diner.

"You shouldn't smoke," I said. "I'm getting Mama to quit because of cancer."

He narrowed his eyes. "She sick?"

"No. And she won't be because I'm making her quit."

"Good girl." He squatted beside me and scratched Noah. "What grade you in now?"

"Fifth. Next month."

He shook his head like it was a wonder. "I bet you've got boyfriends."

"A whole counter full," I said borrowing Mama's line. I sucked in a deep breath but couldn't ask what I needed to know.

He leaned on the railing. "It's good to be back. Sometimes," he said, through a cloud of smoke, "grown-ups need to get away, figure things out." I thought about that, the way Mama talked of moving when things broke. He stroked my hair and said, "I didn't mean to stay away so long," then he flicked his cigarette off the porch and went inside. He didn't feel like my daddy, but I was only three when he left. For years, I pretended he had amnesia, imagining a father-daughter reunion like in the movies. I scrambled up to go inside just as the Magic Fingers Man appeared.

"You're still here?" I asked.

"Yessum." He held the door. "Ready to fix that jukebox?" He was teaching me to be handy.

"Now's not a good time," I said. "Could you come back tomorrow?"

He tilted his head, gave me a look like I was silly, and went inside. I followed, my stomach all prickly. Sheriff Tom was working on his papers and glaring at Wes, who sat spraddle-legged with his back against the counter. He introduced himself as Mama's husband to the Magic Fingers Man.

"Ex-husband," Mama said.

Wes wanted another beer. Mama nodded, so I opened a longneck. Foam bubbled out.

"You're a good helper," Wes said.

"Yes, she is." Mama kissed the top of my head.

"We're celebrating, Magruder," Wes said. "There's a cold one here with your name on it."

"No, thanks."

"He can't drink," I said. "He's an alcoholic." I flushed, avoiding Mama's sharp look. The Magic Fingers Man turned his back. He always told funny stories from his route and let me play the pinballs for free, but today he kept his lips closed tight. Mama poured him a coffee. He thanked her with a smile that looked like it hurt. Tom sat, keeping an eye on everything.

"I've never seen so many folks who don't drink," Wes said, spinning round on his stool.

"Now, why doesn't that surprise me?" Mama said.

Wes leaned over the counter. "We had some fine times, you and me." He grinned, like they had a secret.

"Because I was young and too foolish to know better," she said, wiping away the rings from the other men's cups. He put his hand on hers.

"C'mon, have a beer with me."

"Mama likes lite beer," I said, and hurried round the counter to open one.

"That's how she keeps her figure."

"That and working hard," the Magic Fingers Man said.

Wes ignored him and leaned closer to Mama. "C'mon." His voice was soft and low. She tried not to smile. He grabbed the beers in his left hand and pulled her outside to sit under the shade tree where Mama said we'd picnicked when I was a baby.

I took them a blanket.

"Thanks," Wes said, and winked. He shook it, making a hot breeze, and let it float to the ground. He held Mama's hand while she sat. I started to sit, but Mama told me to sweep up and restock sodas.

I slipped inside real quiet. The Magic Fingers Man turned at the squeak of the screen door. He didn't smile. He asked me not to sweep while he had the Wurlitzer apart. From the window, I watched Mama sitting cross-legged, the beer in her hands. Wes stretched long beside her, leaning on his elbow doing the talking. Mama laughed and shook her head.

"Oh, Lord," Sheriff Tom said, standing behind me.

The Magic Fingers Man joined us, wiping his hands on a red rag. He asked me to fill his spray bottle. He and Tom talked so low I couldn't hear over the faucet.

"I have to retire the Superman pinball, Jessie," he said, though he hadn't finished with the jukebox. "You want to pick the new one? C'mon, I'll show you."

Tom lifted his chin, telling me to go.

Outside, I climbed up into the bed of his truck, squinting against the bright sun. He loosened the tarp and pointed to the machines. "Mars Invasion? Or Vegas Elvis?"

"I don't care," I said with a shrug, though I wanted Elvis. Mama would too.

"Hm. Vegas Elvis then," he said, like he'd read my mind. "Hop in, I need your eyes to help me back around to the ramp."

The hot seat burned the backs of my legs.

"When's the last time you saw your father?" he asked.

"Not since I was a kid." I found Mama and my daddy in the side mirror.

He laughed. "So, a long time ago." He gently poked my side.

"Hey!" I shrieked. I was very ticklish.

"All clear?"

"Yep." My parents got closer in the mirror, and I wondered if they were talking about me.

I rode the tailgate to the ground with Vegas Elvis. The Magic Fingers Man wedged it on the dolly, pushed it over the gravel and up the ramp. Tom offered to help.

"Hold the door?" he grunted.

Wes came over, hands on hips. "Looks like you could use some muscle there."

"No, thanks. I got it," the Magic Fingers Man said, his face red as he pushed.

"Suit yourself," Wes said, and made a funny face that made me laugh, a crazy laugh. Sheriff Tom's look said I'd let him down.

Inside, I rushed to restock soda and beer bottles from the storeroom, carrying too many; a few slipped and crashed on the floor. Mama raced in, Wes behind her.

"What are you doing?" she asked, looking at the mess.

"I'm restocking. Mr. Magruder said I couldn't sweep."

"Just while the jukebox is open," he said. He strode across the floor, lifted me out of the broken glass and beer, set me on a stool and checked my foot. "Jessie's cut herself," he said.

I was surprised to see blood.

"Oh, dear." Mama got the first-aid kit.

"Let me help," Wes said, rounding the counter so fast he slipped and landed in the beer.

"Y'all stay put," Mama said, "until I get this cleaned up."

Wes sat beside me, pulled napkins from the dispenser, and wiped his sleeve. "We're in trouble now," he said, bumping me with his shoulder. I bumped him back. He smelled like smoke and something spicy.

"Sit still," Mama said, gripping my foot. The tweezers pinched, and then she held up a tiny sliver of glass.

"Why is it, Wes," she said, "that whenever you're around there's trouble?"

"I'm just naturally exciting."

Tom's radio squawked, and everyone jumped. Murphy's horse was loose on the 41. Tom sighed and grabbed his hat. He told Wes, "I better not catch you drunk on my highway."

"Still King of the Road?"

Tom leaned close. "Glad to see you haven't forgotten everything."

Wes looked at me and rolled his finger around by his ear. Tom grumbled and headed for the door. Wes lifted my chin.

"Let's see if you're as strong as you are cute, doll." He set his elbow on the counter. I turned and set my elbow next to his.

"Think you can whup me?" he asked.

"I'd sure like to try."

"She's not alone," Mama said.

"You can be next." He gave her a flirty smile.

"Jessie's strong like her mama," the Magic Fingers Man said, switching out songs on the jukebox. I wanted him to hurry up and go.

Wes's hand was hard and scratchy like an old work glove. I pushed as hard as I could. "Oh," he moaned as I slammed his hand to the counter. I flexed my muscles.

He laughed. "How 'bout you, Magruder?"

"You just got whupped by a little girl, it wouldn't seem right."

"I'm almost ten," I reminded him.

"That's right," Wes said. Mama bit her lip, her eyes shifting between the two men. Wes asked if I wanted to meet his dog and pushed up his sleeve to show a bulldog tattoo on his muscle. I leaned in for a closer look and it jumped and barked. My squeak made Wes laugh again. A quarter dropped in the jukebox, and Elvis started singing Mama's favorite: "Blue Suede Shoes."

Mama clapped. "You fixed it!" Magruder offered his hand, but Wes jumped up and pulled her out from behind the counter. She hesitated.

"Mama, dance!" I said.

Wes held her close as they two-stepped around the tables. The Magic Fingers Man watched for a second, then packed up. When the music stopped, "You're Lookin' at Country" started. Wes twirled her around like in the movies. Mama's eyes shone. I wanted a turn. The Magic Fingers Man tapped Wes's shoulder and said, "This one's mine." Mama took his hand. He whispered something I couldn't hear. Her eyes still shone, but he wasn't as fancy a dancer as Wes, who leaned against the wall, working his mouth, watching.

When they finished, she said she had work to do, but he held her hands, his quiet smile asking a question. She shrugged, shook her head, and pulled her hands free. He turned and wheeled the old pinball machine out, but he still felt big in the room. Mama busied herself with the mail.

"Cook's off today," I told Wes, "but I could make you a sandwich."

"Maybe some peanuts." He nodded to the snacks on the shelf by the register and opened his wallet. Inside was a picture of Mama. "That's one beautiful woman," he said. I asked if he had one of me. "She never sent me one," he whispered. I ran upstairs and hurried back with a picture. In it, he and I are smiling big behind the wheel of his rig. I'm just a baby, standing on his lap, steering.

Wes laughed, moaned about how young he looked. "You sure were cute," he said. "But boy, could you holler."

"Is that why you left us?" I asked. I could feel Mama watching.

"Your mama told me to git."

"Wes! Now that's not fair," she said, her voice shaky.

His smile disappeared. "Well, I deserved it, I had some growing up to do." Mama stared, mouth open. "But I'm back and I'm going to make it up to you."

The Magic Fingers Man came back for his toolbox. He set it by the door and asked Mama for a cold Pepper. Outside, a loud motorcycle roared by on the road.

"How 'bout that arm wrestle?" Wes asked.

"C'mon," I said. "It's real fun."

The men stared at each other hard.

"Well," he said, "if Jessie's asking." He sat and turned to Wes. I was surprised by how much bigger he was. His face was quiet and tanned; Wes's flushed and freckled. They locked hands. I counted to three. Right away Wes was losing.

I said, "Go, Daddy," trying it on. Then Wes moved his elbow and slammed their fists to the counter. "Hey!" I said.

Wes sipped his beer. The Magic Fingers Man smiled with half his mouth and didn't say a word. He stood and put change on the counter. Mama said his Pepper was on the house, but he didn't pick it up. She twisted the dishtowel in her hands, then followed him out. Wes asked me who he was.

"He's the Mag—he's Mr. Magruder."

Wes lowered his voice. "Yeah ... but are they ... ?" He rubbed his palms together. "You know?"

I didn't. "He's our friend," I said. I didn't tell him I'd been hoping he could be more. I didn't say I'd seen them kissing.

I pressed my cheek to the hot glass of the diner's window. Mama stood on the porch, hand raised as the flatbed drove off. She stood like that until a dusty station wagon pulled in. All four doors opened at once, spilling kids. The parents leaned on the doors looking wrung out.

I hurried upstairs and dug through Mama's dresser until I found a postcard with a cartoon map of California.

Rosie,

I hope you got my letter. I'm coming home to put things right.

Be there soon.

Love, Wes

Nothing about me. I folded the postcard in my pocket with Carla's letter and went outside.

Mama was telling the station wagon people there was no hot water, but she'd take twelve dollars off the room.

"Be careful with that," I warned the kids, who were climbing on my swing.

"Why?" asked a boy with the biggest ears I ever saw.

"'Cuz it was made by magic fingers." They looked at me like a bunch of fish, breathing through their mouths.

"Whose? Your daddy's?" the boy scoffed.

"I bet you get beat up a lot," I said.

"And I bet you're a bas-turd," said his big sister, a skinny girl with frizzy pigtails. I stared her down. She stuck out her tongue and they ran to #5. Least I had my swing back.

Wes banged through the screen door and strolled around the Roadside checking it out. He combed his hair in one of the diner windows. When he saw me watching he froze like the rabbits when I surprised them out back. Then he smiled big and strode over.

"Nice swing," he said.

I pushed off with my feet. "Mr. Magruder made it. He's real handy."

"That so." His eyes ran over it, like he was hunting out mistakes. I pumped hard, going higher. He watched for a few minutes, then went back inside like I was a disappointment. A red tail screeched riding a thermal over my head, and it was like I was up there looking down at this small girl in a handmade swing in a thirsty tree in the middle of nowhere. I let the hot air blow over me, swinging up, up, until I could see down the street to Carla's old house. I'd been riding by all summer, but it just sat empty, windows staring back saying nobody's home. I could hear Mama and Wes, their voices going up and down as the sun dropped low. Then the noise of the TV in the brats' room, #5, reminded me it was time for our show.

I found Mama sitting on the counter, kissing Wes, who stood between her knees. This was not the father I'd been waiting for. I spun one of the stools, coughed, and pointed to the clock. We never missed 'Dallas'. She told me to go watch by myself. Wes grabbed me and gave my shoulders a squeeze. He smelled like beer and cigarettes.

"You gonna stay?" I asked.

"That's my plan," he said, grinning at Mama as he turned me to the door.

I rode my bike fast as I could down to Carla's. It hurt to see it all shut up. I sat on the porch and picked at its peeling paint watching the sky turn pink. I always saved her letters as long as I could, but today I couldn't wait.

Dear Jessie,

How're things in Texas? Daddy likes being a shrimper, but my mom worries when he's out to sea. She fixed up my room real neat. Guess what? The house next door is for sale! Your mom could buy it, then this place would be perfect!!!

So far, I haven't met any kids my age ...

I let out a whoop. I knew I should wish her lots of friends, but I couldn't, not yet. I read the rest, pretending she was sitting beside me saying the words. I unfolded Wes's postcard. He never wrote to me. I'd hoped for so long and prayed; had Carla pray. But we were fine without him.

Sheriff Tom woke me. "Time to go," he said. "You gave your mama a scare."

The moon was huge. I tried to find the man in it, but he kept disappearing. Tom put my bike in his trunk and asked if I wanted lights and sirens. I said no.

"Guess you've had enough excitement for one day," he said.

When we pulled in, Mama ran down the steps and hauled open my door. "You can't just go off without telling me!" Her breath smelled like beer and cigarettes now too.

"Found her at Carla's," Tom said. He didn't get out.

"Thanks, Tom," Mama said, stroking my hair so hard it hurt. "There's a fresh pot."

"No thanks. Night Jess. Be smart, Rosie," he said, and drove off.

"Why didn't you tell me he wrote us?" I asked, furious.

"I did. Once. You waited for him on the porch for three days."

"Did he ever ask about me?"

Mama hugged me. "He's here now."

I lay listening to the owl hooting, the trucks passing on the road, someone pulled out of our drive. It was too hot to sleep. I climbed out on the roof and counted lights in the distance. Headlights on the highway lit the refrigerator trucks, USPS, Coors, Mike's eighteen-wheeler, and beside those, a tarp-covered flatbed. I tiptoed quickly downstairs and slipped outside.

A light was on in the utility room. Relief flooded through me to see the Magic Fingers Man but then I remembered how mean I'd been.

"Best not flood this place," he said, "or we'll need more new parts." He pointed to his toolbox and asked for a three-quarter-inch wrench, but the numbers on his tools were blurred. He handed me a towel and just let me cry.

"I'm sorry," I said. "About spilling your beans … and … everything."

He gave me a crooked smile. "You and me are just fine."

I wiped my eyes, found the wrench, gave it to him, and sat back against the wall hugging my knees. Moths tapped crazily at the ceiling bulb, fluttered away, dove in again.

"I knew you'd come back," I lied.

"Guess I'm too predictable."

"That's a good thing."

His crooked smile widened. "Well, my special assistant needs hot water, and I just happened to find the right part."

"Does Mama know you're here?"

He pushed his glasses up on his nose. "No."

I scrambled up. "I'll go get her."

"No, no. She's busy now," he said. "And I'm not staying."

That night, I sat for a long time on the cool concrete watching him, his fingers on the tools, making things work.

Wake

Brenna is the only one in this crowded house Molly can stand. The others, dressed in their funeral black, watch to see how she's bearing up but Molly keeps her eyes straight ahead, avoids their faces painted with grief. Faces quick to look away from his handiwork, the black and blue of it reserved for her. Only Brenna is wanted. Brenna who helped her enroll in college courses online at the library, who hid Molly's books in her desk. Once, Brenna touched a bruise on her face with such tenderness, like a butterfly kiss, and Molly's eyes swam with tears. Brenna never asked why she stayed.

The rocking chair Molly sits in was once her grandmother's, then her mother's, meant for soothing and children. The yellow stench of his cigarettes clings to the cushion. Her mother never liked him, warned he'd be trouble—she would know—called him too sweet-talking-to-trust, words Molly mistook for jealousy. After they married, Paul refused her any contact then spent the twelve years until her mother's death proving her right.

Paul's friends from the plant crowd the living room, smoking, lifting glasses, inventing sloppy tributes to a man they knew in high school, not the one she slept beside for fifteen years. They're all quick to offer condolences. But her loss is not him.

She looks beyond them, down the gravel track that leads from the house to the main road, where the mailbox tilts south from its own run-ins with his drunkenness. Molly'd grown to hate the sun's fall to suppertime, listening for the sound of those tires coming home, measuring the bang of the front door to know the evening's weather. No more.

Five nights ago, she lay wide-awake in bed, a box cutter secreted between the mattress and frame. She'd talked back that morning and he left her with a hateful look, his promissory note for what he'd bring home later. But when she woke the next morning, the house was empty. All she heard was birdsong, then the sheriff knocking at the door.

Father Thomas, flushed from heat and Irish, pats the belly that strains the front of his black cassock; he protests as Trudy Johnson hands him another slice of her cake. Trudy smooths her hair, tells him the service was "lovely, just right." For whom? Molly wonders. Only once did Molly dare confess her need to leave Paul, fearing he'd kill her. "Now, now," Father Thomas said, his breath whiskey-sour through the dark confessional screen. "You mustn't let emotions cloud your thinking. Losing that baby was hard, I know." He knew nothing. "These things happen to test our faith." He called it "God's will" and reminded Molly to be "subject in everything to your husband to achieve a state of grace." Be silent in the flock, he meant, be fixed like a prie-dieu for Paul to kneel on.

Molly never returned to the confessional. She only went to Sunday mass when Paul insisted, when he bowed his head and passed the plate, his face a mask for God and town. She wondered if Paul ever confessed, his hands still throbbing from the work of ensuring her salvation. What penance did Father Thomas assign to him?

As if hearing Molly's thoughts, the priest's eyes beneath ragged brows catch hers and widen. He looks away, tugs at his Roman collar; when he looks back, he's donned his made-for-mourning face. She turns her gaze back to the window, down her drive to the flat horizon. A bleak view she'd once confused with beauty.

She counts the footsteps of people passing in and out her door under Jesus on the cross. She counts the minutes until they leave. Steady counts to match her pulse, the rhythm of that something still alive, long hidden inside her.

Drifting voices complain about the weather as if today should be anything but hot. Women shoo the striped cat Molly feeds on the sly, a creature with enough sense to keep its distance from him. She wants to tell them to let the cat be, but she's too practiced in silence. Alice Barnes puts it out and Molly remembers how the cat arched its spine and hissed at Paul, how he'd fallen, hard, after he'd drunkenly tried to kick it. Her laughter is a high, sharp sound that slows their chatter. They expect her to be miserable and invent more empty words to stir the fury that howls inside her. Molly rocks, wishing they'd go, take their simpering sympathies with them. They just came to sniff around, for free cake and booze she wouldn't have offered.

Sheriff Jake, Paul's friend, told her not to worry about the insurance, that it was "taken care of," meaning he'd whitewashed the DUI, the only help he'd ever given. Only once did she make the mistake of calling him for protection, a call she'd barely lived to regret.

The good sheriff drinks only coffee, he's "on duty", but she's seen him tipping the whiskey bottle over his cup. The cup he sets without a saucer on her white tablecloth, the one her mother made so long ago when Molly was new, and her mother collected a future for her in a "hope chest." She feels the dark ring his cup burns into the delicate lace, another painful stain.

Outside, the striped cat stretches in the hot sun, rolls in the gravel, wrestles with unseen demons. Molly's hands ache from clenching, from twisting the wedding band she longs to fling off. It's hard to breathe with these people, his people she's lived beside, an outsider all her married life.

Paul's foreman from the plant lumbers out the door, across her porch, over the treasure she's been collecting for fourteen years. Pennies and nickels, dollars and fives, scrimped from her meager grocery allowance, from his pockets, or his wallet the nights he passed out, too drunk to remember what he'd spent. The cat jumps as the foreman's boots thump past. Molly is proud of the way she ruffles her fur and flees.

Brenna crouches her thin body beside the rocking chair. Her touch so gentle, so soft on Molly's wrist, it feels foreign.

"Need anything?" she asks, her tired eyes full of questions.

"Open a window?" Molly says. "Please?"

"Don't worry," she whispers. "They'll go soon." Molly's throat tightens, and she squeezes Brenna's hand, wanting to share with her everything that is good and true.

Brenna pounds her fist against the frame, forces the window open, and lets a breeze into the room, to lift all the history that dusts the surfaces of this narrow place. His house. Now hers.

The priest saunters over to her.

She stops rocking, says, "I need fresh air."

They all watch with open pity, glasses poised. Hands seize her arms to help her up, as if she's ancient but she's only thirty-two. She shudders out of their grip and hurries through the gap they make in the smoke-stale room where from this day forward no one will smoke again.

She slips out the door, eases it closed and hurries down her stairs, beyond their view, as a butterfly flutters its orange wings in a labored spiral up, up, into the cobalt sky above her sun-warmed square of earth. She spreads her arms. The heat of the sun on her face is a power she longs to harness, to set the world on fire, starting here.

Abundance

A car honked—shave and a haircut—outside my bedroom window. In the driveway, a man in a rumpled brown suit climbed out of a gray Chevelle and leaned against it, smoking and squinting against the harsh sunlight. It wasn't until Colin flew out of the house that I knew the man was Colin's father, their relation evident in their freckles, their short, wiry bodies, their irritable cowlicks. Colin threw his arms around the man, jumping up and down, making him stagger. He grabbed Colin's shoulders, held him at arm's length, and said something I couldn't hear. I cranked open the window, letting in the California chill of December with the bitter stink of ivy.

"Who's that?" my big sister Katie asked, joining me at the window. Little Rose elbowed in between us.

"Colin's dad."

He was strange, like someone from 'The Twilight Zone', nothing like the man Colin bragged about: "My dad could take anybody. He's got Charles Atlas muscles." My sisters shared a wide-eyed look, and then Rose raced for the door. Katie followed.

"C'mon, Joan," they called. But I waited, my excitement that Colin was finally leaving overtaken by the sharp regret that I hadn't kept my promise, hadn't been his Joan of Arc. I checked myself in the mirror, hating the thick braid Mother did for mass, as if pulling my hair tight and straight could tame me.

When I ran out to the driveway, my father was shaking the man's hand and calling him Ray. I hurried to take my place in the lineup of my siblings, tallest to shortest, oldest to youngest, as my father said our names: "Dennis, Katie, Stevie, Joan, Rose—" He looked around for one more. "And Danny." He pointed to the newest of us on Mother's hip, chewing on her blouse, but she didn't seem to notice. She was taking Ray's measure as he counted, bobbing his head along our line the way people did. Ray told Colin he was lucky to have so many kids to play with. Stevie muttered behind his fist, "Those are Charles Atlas muscles?"

Mother was still in her nice church skirt and the blue blouse that matched her eyes. She'd put on lipstick and looked pretty, the way she'd looked before Colin came and made her so tired.

"Happy New Year!" Ray's voice was rough, smoky. "1964!" He shook his head like time was a mystery, then yelled into the car, "Get out here and say hello to your brother."

The passenger door squeaked open and a girl climbed out. Colin's sister. Pale hair swung loose at her shoulders. My sisters and I weren't allowed to wear ours down—"It makes a girl look loose"—Mother said, but this girl clinging to the door handle looked tied up in knots. Her long legs ended in high-heeled black plastic sandals; she already had breasts. She and Colin eyed each other, shoulders hunched. They didn't hug, just smiled shyly, and pushed at each other's arms as if testing whether the other was real.

Ray leaned against his battered car and answered Father's questions about his drive while Colin's sister studied her sandals, her feet bulging around too tight straps.

"You must be Laura," Mother said. The girl looked so uncomfortable it made my bones itch. "You're twelve?"

Laura nodded.

"Joan's eleven. Katie's thirteen." Laura's eyes slid over my skinny frame, Katie's pudge, our matching church dresses, and braids. She sidled up to Ray, clutching his arm as he opened the trunk of his car.

"Let go of me, girl," he snapped. "I gotta get Colin's presents."

Colin raced to Ray's side as the man lifted a bike with a red bow from the trunk, revealing more presents wrapped in Christmas paper and stacked on a jumble of rags and boxes with crushed corners. Laura took one of the presents, hugged it to her chest, and stared at the driveway like it had her in a trance.

Colin danced around his father, pointing at Dennis and Stevie, shouting, "Look what my dad brought me! I told ya." Stevie's smile was a grimace. Colin tried to ride the bike but toppled over. It was too big for his nine-year-old frame. Mother set Danny down for once and went to help him, holding the bicycle and offering soft encouragement until he steadied and rode alone down the driveway to the sidewalk.

"We expected you on Christmas," Mother said. She lifted Danny back onto her hip. Ray's smile disappeared under her withering gaze. I was awed that Mother's force extended to this grown man. Ray shoved his hands in his pockets like Colin did when he was in trouble. "He waited," Mother said, her voice level. "All day."

Ray rocked on the balls of his feet and mumbled that he got tied up. I imagined him bound up in ropes.

Colin yelled, "Look, Dad! Look!"

"Get a load of that," Ray said, hands on hips, shaking his head like he'd never seen a person ride a bike before. Colin pedaled back and forth on the sidewalk, then raced back up the driveway, nearly hitting me.

"Git outta my way," he snarled.

I waited for Mother to scold him, but she praised him, just for riding a bike. She put her hand on Laura's shoulder and invited her into the house. Ray and Father followed. Colin leaned his bike against the brick planter on the porch.

"Don't touch it," he warned, and ran inside.

I stood with my brothers and sisters looking at that bike, its shiny blue frame, the handle grips with multi-colored streamers. None of us ever had one brand-new. Mine was a hand-me-down from Sister Agnes Lucille, a black three-speed with a weird bubbled bump on the fender like the wart on her wrist.

"Big deal," Dennis said. "His dad's still a drunk."

I kicked the front tire, rubbing dirt into its pure white sidewall.

We settled into the living room, crowded with the Christmas tree. Laura was entranced by the nativity scene, touching all the pieces that Mother said were only for looking. Ray told Colin to open his presents. There were none for us. Colin unwrapped a Sears garage and other fancy toys from TV, the kind Father said were cheap, a waste of money—the toys we all wanted. I watched, trying to smile, pretending it was Christmas again, reliving the disappointment.

"Aren't you lucky," Mother said as Colin showed off new roller skates. Katie smoothed and folded the wrapping paper, earning Mother's smiling approval. I wished I'd thought of that.

"Your sister saved one of hers to open with you," Ray told Colin.

Laura, who still hadn't said a word, unwrapped the gift clutched tightly in her hands; an art set, the thing I'd most wanted. It opened like a suitcase, with rainbows of paper, pencils, and paints. I gasped, filled with envy so strong Mother must have felt it, because she told me to help her in the kitchen.

I sliced apples while Mother arranged the last of the Christmas cookies on a large paper doily. "Jealousy," she said, "is unchristian and unbecoming in a lady."

"But it's what I wanted."

Her eyes rested on me, but her sad look was far away. She sighed and said, "Maybe for your birthday." She told me I should be happy for Colin whose parents never sent him anything, and I cringed, remembering a day three months earlier.

Rose and I were in the small backyard, sitting on the patchy lawn making daisy chains, when Colin appeared with a rumpled paper bag full of candy. He peeled foil off a Hershey bar, scenting the air with chocolate. I salivated as he bit off a large piece.

"Where'd you get that?" I asked, plucking up grass.

"At the store." Brown smeared across his big front teeth.

"Where'd you get the money?"

"My dad." He sat on his shins, squinting behind his smudged glasses.

"Yeah, right."

"Yeah, huh. He sent me ten bucks."

"Bet you stole it," I said. "Better share or we'll tell."

"No way."

Rose pointed her Barbie at him. "You're supposed to share."

"Okay, share your dolly," he said, and grabbed Barbie. Rose yanked her back and Barbie's head popped off. Rose shrieked. Colin scrambled to his feet, laughing, Barbie's glossy yellow hair squished between his grubby fingers. We chased him through the narrow side yard out to the busy street, but he was too fast. Rose told the boys when they got home, waving headless Barbie as evidence. Then

Stevie discovered his paper route money was missing. Again.

We cornered Colin by the garage, behind the clothesline hung with white sheets shielding us from Mother's view. He backed away, hands clenched, face twitching. Stevie slapped a fist into his palm and demanded his money as we forced Colin into the ivy-choked fence.

Rose said, "You owe me a new doll, ugly head." She was fierce, her hair copper in the sun.

Colin smirked. "Ha-ha. Didn'tdoitdidn'tdoit." Diapers flapped overhead, smelling of bleach in the hot wind.

"No wonder his parents don't want him," Stevie muttered. I sucked in my breath, shocked to hear him say out loud what I'd thought myself.

"I smell shit," Dennis said. Sometimes Colin still pooped his pants. Dennis helped Stevie pin him down, a scramble of skinny arms and legs. Stevie searched his pockets but found only coins, a plastic soldier, and Barbie's head.

"Dang you," Stevie said. Dennis yanked up Colin's shirt and thrust a crumbly piece of charcoal at me. Fingers shaking, I wrote rat on his belly as he kicked and squirmed.

"I hate you," Colin said.

"Yeah? Well, we double hate you," Stevie said. His face reddened; hate was the most forbidden word. He pulled his baseball cap low.

"I'm telling Mommy."

"She's not your mommy," I said.

The slam of the back door scattered us like buckshot. I ran to the woodpile and hid. Triumph turned to a miserable shame in my belly. I rubbed the charcoal from my fingers, but no matter how much I spat I couldn't wash the black away. I wondered if God was watching me, an evil, wild thing. I tried to imagine waiting for someone to claim me when no one ever did. It made me feel hollowed out, queasy from my sins of hatred, for praying he'd leave, run away, even die. I scratched my knee and picked a scab until it bled. I'd confessed my sin of hating him over and over in the dark confessional, done my penance of Hail Marys and Our Fathers, tried to be loving and kind, but it never lasted.

I arranged the apple slices like a flower, the way Mother liked, understanding that Colin was finally leaving, that it was too late to be the person I'd meant to be. I wondered how he'd remember me, what he'd say about me to his sister. Father came into the kitchen and said Ray wanted coffee. Mother scooped Folgers into the percolator and asked how Ray could afford all those gifts.

"He sold his life insurance."

"He had life insurance?" Mother said, surprised.

"Yes." Father lowered his voice. "But no place to live." He leaned on the counter. "He's living out of his car." Mother made a prune mouth. I wondered if the backseat was Laura's room and imagined a long trip, my father all to myself. "He sold his only asset for all that sorry crap." Father flung his arm wide, his voice raspy with anger. I waited for Mother's comment about his language, but she just shook her head, set the apples and cookies on a tray, and handed it to me.

"Go pass this around." She retied the sash on the back of my dress and nudged me to the door. "Try to be good." I lingered long enough to hear Father say that Laura was with Ray because she'd been thrown out of her foster home.

"Why?"

"The mother said she was a slut."

"But the girl is only twel—. Oh, dear," Mother said. "Where will she go?"

"Maybe that's why he's here."

"No!" I spun around, and a cookie flew from the tray. Mother tsked, picked up the pieces, and shooed me out.

In the living room, someone had turned on the football game. Probably Colin showing off the color TV, a gift from Father Angelis. It was all that priest's fault. He convinced my parents to take Colin, promising it was just a visit, "a few months" while Colin's father got straight, and his mother found her mental bearings. My parents called a family meeting and we all crowded into their bedroom. Mother settled into her rocking chair beside the crib. She said it was a family decision, and then she told us about a little boy's sorry life: a father addicted to whiskey, a mother locked up in a mental ward, how when this little boy was bad his parents left him out alone in the dark all night and when he pooped his pants, they rubbed his nose in it, like a dog. My whole body hurt as I listened to every horrible detail. Mother ran her hands over her pregnant belly. Father leaned against the dresser; his eyes followed her hands.

"Can't he go somewhere else?" Dennis dared ask.

Mother sighed and spoke to the Blessed Virgin on her dresser. "I don't see how we can say no."

I agreed, vowing to Jesus that I'd love him and be his protector like my namesake, Saint Joan of Arc.

Colin was seven when Father Angelis brought him to "visit" two years ago. I tried hard those first weeks, smiling, full of sympathy, my heart on tiptoe, imagining his homesick sorrow. But Colin was not easy to love. He was sullen and mean, with a twitchy freckled face, and he hated everyone.

School started a month later. We all went together. The boys and Katie ran ahead to the upper school; Rose skipped behind, hand-in-hand with her best friend. But I walked with Colin as I'd promised Mother, sack lunches and Pee-Chee folders clutched in our hands. Colin's new shoes had an irritating squeak that added to my first-day jitters. I told him I was nervous, too.

"Really?" He looked doubtful.

I told him about recess and showed him the asphalt playground and jungle gym. At the principal's office, I patted his shoulder and said, "Well—"

He just blinked, his freckles twitching.

"I hope you make a friend."

"Don't go!" he pleaded, fists balled, but the warning bell rang. I pointed to the clock, shrugged an apology, and left him, relief easing my guilt.

Colin started in second grade with Rose, who told me about his trips to Mother Superior and his "accidents." He was soon put down to first. And he had other troubles: smashing windows, fighting, stealing, breaking Rose's front teeth. Through it all he bragged about his father—"way taller than your dad"—who was coming to get him any day. As the months turned to years, I began to pray for the threatened visit.

I served the apples and cookies, then set the tray on the coffee table. Laura crouched silently beside Ray, twisting her fingers in the carpet, scratching at the bottom as if for hidden treasure. I squished on the sofa between Katie and Rose, who whispered that maybe Laura was a crazy, too.

"Yeah, well, she might be moving into our room," I whispered back.

"Liar," Rose said, and looked at Colin's sister with alarm.

Laura's hair was greasy. She had a dreamy, faraway look, but her long dark lashes and pale hands were mesmerizing; her fingers fluttered, so expressive, though she didn't say a word. I wondered, if she stayed, whether the kids at Immaculate Heart would like her better than me.

Mother said, "Why don't you girls take Laura to play in your room?"

I groaned. I hated the way kids looked at our three beds, everything jammed too close. Still, I invited her, but Laura stayed put.

"We could draw," I said. Laura gripped her art set and narrowed her eyes.

"Or play a game?" Rose said.

"Go on." Ray gave Laura a push. She stood. His eyes moved up and down her legs. She tugged on her short dress two sizes too small.

"We got 'Sorry' for Christmas," Katie said as Laura followed us down the hall to the bedroom. "Wanna play?"

"We have to start again anyway," I said. "Colin kicked our game over before you came."

Laura finally spoke, her voice a soft chime. "Doesn't matter," she said. "I'm gonna leave any minute." I wondered if she really had no idea and squatted to pack up the game spilled across the narrow space of floor. Rose perched with Katie on my bed. Where did my parents think Laura would sleep? She stood before the mirror above our wide, sagging dresser, whose drawers opened only with a fight. It couldn't hold anything more. She lifted our snow globe from Nana Ann and tilted it back and forth, making it storm. I fought the urge to snatch it away. She touched our saint figurines and my bottle cap collection, picking things up in her long fingers and putting them down. She shook her dirty hair off her pale face and stared at herself in the mirror like she was seeing a ghost.

"Do you have a pen pal?" I asked. "We could write."

Laura's eyes met mine and looked right through me as if she already knew everything she needed to know. She turned back to the mirror, told her reflection, "I'd never want to live here," and walked out.

"Well, who asked you?" I said, and jumped up, moving around the bedroom mimicking Laura, acting dim, touching things, staring crazy into the mirror. My sisters laughed hysterically, then went silent. Katie coughed. Mother stood in the doorway, and her look sliced me in two.

"Can't you show some Christian kindness to that poor girl? You disappoint Jesus." I stiffened and rubbed my fingers on my church dress.

Katie and Rose followed Mother out, but I planted myself in the doorway where the pink linoleum of my bedroom met the rust-colored carpet of the hall. I knew Mother was right. Still, an angry worm of jealousy twisted in my stomach when I thought of that art set, the new bike, my mother always taking other people's sides. The hum of the football game and voices drifted down the hall, which still smelled of after-church bacon. Mother was telling Ray about Colin's new glasses, the nine fillings he'd needed, his First Communion. I braced a foot into either corner of the doorway, gripped the jambs in my hands, and leaned into the dark hallway, then back into my crowded, sunlit bedroom. Back and forth, like a punching clown, dark and light, back and forth, furious. My braid snapped my spine, stinging. I unwound it, shook it all loose. A shiver ran over my scalp as I bent and swept the floor with my hair, side to side, certain in that moment that I could never be the other, better Joan.

"What are you doing?" Mother peered down the hall at me from the living room. "Come join us," she said as if it were an invitation to fun. She was holding Danny in her lap, as usual. Her eyes narrowed at my hair hanging loose to my waist. Father was in his chair, silent, in the quiet place he went when feelings were up. He looked warm and soft in his new flannel shirt from Christmas. I wanted to sit with him, but he turned me to the crowded couch. I perched on its arm against the scratchy Christmas tree, dried up and shedding needles.

"Dr. Shrier," Mother said, "thinks Colin's getting better. He's the psychiatrist." She whispered the word, each syllable a separate sin. Welfare paid that bill.

Colin sat on the floor in the middle of the circle of our two families, his legs bent under him. He clutched the carpet as if the house might suddenly lift and spin like Dorothy's on her tornado ride to Oz. He stared with such longing at Ray that I wondered what he saw. To me, Ray looked like something wrung flat through our roller iron. He hadn't shaved. Tiny red lines like on a gas station map covered his face. He sat on the edge of a straight-backed chair, some part of him always moving as if everything itched.

"So," he said, his strained smile revealed a gap on the side where two teeth should have been. "I hope the kid's been behavin' hisself."

"He tries," Mother said, eyes soft on Colin. Her mouth formed a small lipstick smile like she had nothing but Virgin Mary love for him. Father told how Colin was getting real good at baseball now that he had glasses.

Colin bobbed his head. "Yeah," he said. "I been good, Dad." As if it would make a difference. The hope in his face hurt my stomach. Katie nudged me as Colin picked his nose.

"Ugh, Colin, don't," I said. Mother snapped a finger into the back of my head. But who would want him if he kept doing that?

"That girl's right," Ray said. "No sense digging where you won't find gold." He laughed, alone. He coughed. "I can't get over you in glasses. Do the kids call you Four Eyes?"

Colin scowled. He pushed his glasses up his nose. "I hate 'em," he said, and shot a quick look at Stevie and Dennis, who sat silent, slack-jawed, hypnotized by a beer commercial on TV. Ray bent to light a cigarette with a quivering match. He inhaled deeply.

"Have you found work?" Father asked as he handed Mother, then Ray, a cup of coffee.

"Well, I sure been looking," Ray said. "There's a job up in Hayward at an auto parts I might get."

Father made his humming sound that meant he didn't believe it, then slipped back to the kitchen. Ray's hands shook; ash spilled down his shirt. He puckered his lips, his face scrunched like he was in pain as he lifted the cup to his mouth. He slurped, then jumped, spilling coffee on the carpet.

"Sorry," he mumbled. "Hot." I looked at the spill, anticipating Mother's inevitable comment that she could never have anything nice.

"Someone get a towel," she said, but I was already running to the kitchen, where Father stood staring out the small window over the sink. I wrapped my arms around him.

"Ray spilled," I said. Father's belly rose and fell against my cheek. "Is Colin leaving?"

"Doesn't look like it." My heart sank. He patted my back.

"Hurry up, Joan," Mother called.

"Go on," Father said, and pushed me off as if surprised to find me so close.

I knelt at Ray's feet, blotting coffee. His brown shoes tapped, a corner of one sole flapping loose. Laura crouched beside him like a cat, staring into the carpet.

Father leaned in the doorway, drinking his coffee. Ray jerked his head at Laura.

"I'm really trying to get things together. I just need to get the girl settled first," he said, eyes swerving like Colin's did when he lied. "But it's gonna take time."

I wanted to ask why almost three years wasn't enough. And now he wanted to dump Laura on us too?

"Laura's a good girl," he said. "God knows I want them with me, but I got to get things—straight." He ran his hand through what was left of his hair. "Just for a little while." He looked right at me as if I had any say.

Mother's brow creased, her eyes darting from Father to Laura to Ray. "Oh, I don't think—"

"We've got our hands full, Ray," Father said.

Mother suggested calling our pastor. Danny crawled off her lap and hid behind her. She shifted to the edge of her seat, hands on knees, shoulders high. "I'm sure he'll help," she said. Her eyes flicked to Laura like she owed the girl something but Laura turned her cool gaze on me.

Colin fidgeted, a tic in his cheek kept a jittery beat. "I'm going with you, Dad," he said. "I'm going with you. Right, Dad? Right?"

My hands clenched. I wanted to scream at him to shut up, tell him he wasn't going anywhere, but the only one talking was the football announcer on TV.

Ray wiped his nose on his sleeve. Father coughed, put a hand on Ray's shoulder, and told him to buck up. "For the kids." He handed Ray a napkin and took his cup to the kitchen. I'd never seen a grown man cry. Ray blew his nose and wiped his eyes. Laura clutched her art set, her eyes darting slyly between Mother and Ray.

"Laura, dear," Mother said. "I'm so sorry." It unnerved me to see Mother nervous, her neck flushed, her hands busy at her skirt. "We'll call Father Angelis."

"What could he do?" Laura's eyes were hard as she pointed at Colin, proving her point.

Father returned with Ray's cup, wafting a whiskey smell.

"Dear?" Mother looked angry.

"Just one." Father's jaw was set, so she didn't argue. Ray clutched the cup like a prayer and drank it down in two gulps. He rolled it in his hands, then set it down and sat a little taller.

"This is a real nice place you got here," he said. Father nodded, said thanks. Ray looked at his watch, stood, and put on his coat.

"Wait!" Colin jumped up and raced down the hall.

"Ray!" Mother said. "You aren't leaving?"

He didn't answer. Laura hugged the art set to her chest. Colin tore back into the room and stuffed his old duffel with his gifts.

"Stay a little longer," Father said, his face pained. "Let us make some calls."

But Ray moved to the front door fast, like he might break into a run, Laura stuck to his side. His hand shook on the doorknob.

Outside, he jangled his keys, looking up at the blue sky, then down at the driveway.

Colin dragged his duffel out the door, panting. "Dad. Wait for me."

"Hey," Ray said, his face twitching. "It's just a few more weeks. Maybe a month." He shook Colin's hand. "You're doin' good here. I just can't get over you in glasses." His laugh was sharp, metallic. Tears stung my eyes as Colin began to cry. "Hey now, don't do that, be a man. What about that bike?"

"He's just a kid!" I cried, my heart wild in my chest. Everyone stared at me. I wanted to shout that Ray was a stupid drunk, but it was his job to love Colin.

Laura scuttled into the car, locked her door, and slid low in her seat. Ray shoved his hands in his pockets, swaying from foot to foot, his eyes everywhere but on Colin.

"Be good," he said, and jumped into his car. The engine knocked twice before sputtering to an idle. Colin reached in the window.

"Take me. I'll be good," he begged. "I promise."

Ray rolled up his window. Father cursed and told everyone to go back inside.

"Colin, come away from that car," Mother called from the porch. "Why would he even want to go with that man?" she asked Father, who didn't answer. But I knew. I hadn't kept my promise, had never loved him like I should.

"Get inside!" Father shouted. Everyone obeyed except me. I watched Ray's car back down the driveway, Colin running alongside, grabbing the handle, Ray reaching up to lock his door, the car backing into the road, Colin racing up the driveway with the bulging duffel banging against his side, throwing his leg over his too tall bike, pushing off, unsteady at first, then pedaling full out after his family down the middle of the street while Ray's car shrank into the distance and out of sight.

"Colin!" I took off after him, my shoes slapping against the asphalt. His bike wobbled and fell. A car honked and swerved around him. Colin stood slowly, like an old man, his eyes fixed down the road. I picked his bike up from the ground, spit on the hem of my church dress, and wiped the smudge from the sidewall on his tire, spit and wiped, until it was pure white again.

War Paint

Bennett sucks in a deep breath and knocks. He's not ready for his sister. He eyes the spiny cactus and shudders as the massive oak door swings wide. Cassie's dressed for Thanksgiving in a long brown skirt and buckled shoes. She looks happy to see him, gives him a quick hug but the first thing out of her mouth is, "Where's Margo?"

"She couldn't come." He knows what she's thinking: *Little brother fucked up. Again.*

Lily steps out from behind Cassie. She's six, in red cowboy boots and an orange ruffled dress. "Hi Uncle Bennett," she says and wraps her chubby arms around his legs. He's ridiculously pleased. He gives her the airplane wings the flirty flight attendant gave him.

"Who's Margot?" Lily asks, considering the gift.

"Bennett's girlfriend," Cassie says.

Lily giggles. Cassie asks what happened with Margot. Her hair, once a dark curly mop like Lily's, is now straight and the color of the cashews their mother kept in a bowl in the living room, though he can't remember ever having company. Lines fan from the corners of her eyes, another way she's changed. Bennett extends the box of chocolates, shakes it.

"What that?" Lily asks.

"Lilac chocolates, your mom's favorite."

Cassie thanks him. Hugs the box to her chest with a pitying smile. "No, our mom's favorite."

"No. They were your favorite." An argument brews in his head as he follows her inside. She always confuses the facts. Smells of turkey and sage fill Cassie's kitchen; pots steam on the eight-burner stove. She leads him into the dining room where orange candles flank a cornucopia stuffed with fruits and nuts at the center of a long table. Turkeys on pipe-cleaner legs hold place cards in their beaks. He feels the ache of losing her; Cassie used to be amazing. After college she moved to Brooklyn, worked as a bartender, and painted. Bennett's garage band played a few of her parties full of poets, painters, and pot. He'd wanted to be just like her.

Cassie removes a plate. Margot's, and her ultimatum rings in his ears.

"You said only family," Bennett says, indicating the nine remaining places.

"It's just a few friends."

"But we're supposed to finalize plans for Dad's trip."

"I said we'd talk about it," she says but her face is a no.

"Cassie. Don't fight me on this. I need some time. With him. At home … New York." He has more to say, but Lily pulls him into the cavernous living room, all timber and stone. Kenny G's on the stereo. Pumpkins line the mantel over a fire snapping a temper tantrum; outside it's over sixty degrees. On the L-shaped sofa, a blond wearing a short dress and large turquoise cross sips a pink martini. Beside her a big brunette with lacquered lashes nurses a baby. They smile, look him over like they know his secrets.

Cassie's husband calls hello from the bar at the end of the room and pours him a scotch. "Happy Thanksgiving," he says.

"You too, Jason." Bennett sips. "Bless you, my son," he says, making the sign of the cross. "What are we drinking?" Not that he cares. He's not a big drinker, usually sticks to beer or wine, but on this day he welcomes alcohol's bite.

"Laphroig eighteen."

"Ah, the perks of the cyber guru." Bennett figures it cost two-hundred bucks. Jason developed an elaborate security algorithm he sold to General Dynamics; a self-made man. He's skinny in a sporty way—he rides bikes. His turkey sweater is identical to one Cassie sent Bennett, more evidence that the heat and homogeneity of Scottsdale have warped her. "You," Bennett says, indicating the sweater, "are a good man."

"Where's yours?" Jason asks.

Bennett feigns regret. He likes his brother-in-law, the steady ship in their troubled waters. "I left it in New York." As far as he knows the homeless man at Park and 65th is still wearing it.

Two men amble over and take stools at the bar. Introductions are made.

"You're the musician," booms Peewee, a monster with a buzz-cut block of a head. A former linebacker for the Cardinals, now in sales; he grips Bennett's shoulder as they shake hands.

"Guilty."

"My brother-in-law's a musician by night," Jason says, "songwriter in advertising by day." It sounds like an apology. He asks about Bennett's new album, covers of jazz standards, as Cassie slips under his arm.

"I can't wait to hear it," she says, her voice high.

"Thanks." Bennett shrugs. "People like to live in the past."

The other guy's short and bald with tortoiseshell glasses, a sports-entertainment lawyer. He spouts stats about the Cardinals and crushes Bennett's hand. He indicates Bennett's clothes. "Is it a law New Yorkers have to wear black?"

"It's in the manual," Bennett says. Everyone laughs. Cassie exhales.

"Where's Cassie's drink?" the lawyer asks. She shakes her head. She's born again, not as smart this time.

"Did you meet my bride, Ashley?" Peewee gestures to the sofa.

"Hey there!" Ashley lifts her pink martini. She has a Southern accent. Her eyes crinkle when she smiles. Bennett had paired them by size, but the big brunette, whose lashes make her look startled, belongs to the short lawyer. Something tugs on Bennett's pant leg, a kid wiping his bubbling nose. Peewee scoops him up and plops him beside Ashley. Bennett rubs his trousers with a napkin, smearing the slime.

"Sorry about that," Ashley says. Her hair is fifty shades of blond.

"No problem." Bennett drinks deeply, drowning the panic that always threatens to undo him on fourth Thursdays in November. "Where's Dad?"

"Upstairs," Cassie says. Something beeps in the kitchen and she hurries off.

"How's my dad doing?" Bennett asks.

"Fine. You know him." Jason adds softly, "He doesn't talk about it but he's been reminiscing about New York."

"He's excited about visiting me."

Jason frowns, runs his fingers through his hair laced with silver. "Well … he and Cassandra miss your mother today." He hesitates. "I'm sure you do too."

"Nope." Bennett doesn't miss her. Not her chaos and swings, not the cruel way she left them. "It's Dad I miss." He can't miss what he never had. Cassie misses her because when she was a kid their mother was only crazy-lite. She insists Mom was fine when Bennett was little, that she doted on him, but Cassie conflates facts with wishes, her memories with his. The doctors said something switched in his mother's brain after he was born. Cradle-to-grave blame. He gives himself a mental slap. Self-pitying asshole: twenty-nine, alone, snot on your slacks in the goddamn desert. Blub-blub.

He begged Margot to come with, but she lifted her chin and said, "What's the point? It's family only." Two days ago, she gave him an ultimatum: husband or bachelor—choose. The fear of losing her spins him up. He can't imagine his life without her. He needs a smoke, but Cassie disapproves now, not in her home and never in front of her child.

He was ten, Cassie seventeen, the first time their mother was arrested. They waited at the police station, on a bench beside a man handcuffed to its leg, reeking of urine, and begging Bennett to "go get us some hooch" while a woman in a rhinestone sweatsuit paced and yelled at her tattooed daughter slumped on the floor. But it was the fear in his dad's eyes that frightened him most that day, the way he rushed in, hunched, and apologizing, talking low to the cops, paying cash. When a blond in a mink was escorted into the waiting area, she gave the cops the finger. Bennett didn't recognize his mother—a redhead that morning—until she threw her arms wide and cried, "My babies!" Later, in the park, Cassie said, "Mom got caught stealing." Bennett told her, "Moms don't steal." She let him have a cigarette atop Umpire Rock and taught him to inhale. When he coughed, she patted his back and said, "Hurts good." He thought she knew everything. She left for college two months later.

Bennett silences Kenny G, sits at the Steinway no one plays, runs his fingers over the keys, and escapes into the certainty of octaves. Lily climbs up beside him. He tries to teach her "Happy Birthday." She plays loudly, her own arrangement, belting out, "Happy turkey to you ..." like a blues singer, making him laugh until Cassie blows in from the kitchen to shush her, an apron completing her pilgrim look.

"It's fine," Bennett says. "She's improvising." But Cassie sends Lily to watch a video with Peewee's snot-nosed kid. Lily gives him a mournful look and trudges down the hall. "What's with you?" he asks. "The Cassie I knew would have loved that."

She closes her eyes, sways, plops down beside him.

"Are you okay?" he asks and plays a soft riff that always calms him.

"I hate this day."

"Me too. So why do we celebrate it?"

She looks surprised. "Well …" For a moment she drifts off, then says so softly he has to stop playing to hear, "We can't let it be about Mom's death forever. I'm trying to make the Thanksgiving we never had. For Lily. Dad too."

"But you're so uptight."

"It's a lot of work. And I can't think with all that noise."

"Okay then." He closes the piano, stands. She pulls him back down.

"Don't be like that."

"Where's Dad?" He's the reason Bennett's even here.

"I told you. Upstairs. He's napping. Let him rest."

"Don't move," he says and walks to the bar, tops up his drink, and pours a glass of wine for Cassie. He sits. They click glasses.

"Happy Thanksgiving?" she says.

"To Mom, who fucked it all up." They drink in silence and watch Cassie's friends talk.

"Play it for me," she says. He plays the song he wrote for her years ago. Cassie leans against him. For a moment he's glad he came. "Did you and Margot break up?"

He keeps playing. Everyone loves Margot. The opposite of his mother. He closes his eyes, sees her dancer's body pirouette in their apartment, her big green eyes glittering, as if she is made for joy. What would he be without her? Cassie pats his knee and sits on the sofa with Jason. Bennett plays all Cassie's favorites. Ashley claps after each song. He plays 'Stardust', then closes the piano, grabs the wine bottle, and refills Cassie's glass. She tries to stop him.

"Come on, Cassandra," Ashley drawls. "You deserve it."

Cassie shares an eye roll with the big brunette who's burping her bald baby and keeping a wary eye on Bennett. She's drinking Diet Coke and hasn't said a word. Her bald husband wraps an arm around her, marking his territory. Bennett sits on the hearth among cancerous-looking gourds.

"I'm sorry Margot couldn't come," Jason says, voicing Bennett's longing.

"She's getting a PhD in psychology," Cassie says. "She's smart, beautiful, and wants children."

Margot does want kids, with him. That's the problem. But he couldn't do that to her. Not on his DNA. She isn't worried, but he's done the research. He could pass the crazy on; he has a thirty-percent chance of going nuts himself.

"He'll lose her if he drags his feet," Cassie says.

"Here's an idea," Bennett says. "Mind your own business?"

"Whoa." Peewee tucks his chin, doubling it. Bennett flushes, checks his watch; hours to go.

Jason says, "Peewee and Ashley just celebrated ten years!" Peewee tells how he met Ashley in college while volunteering on Bush's campaign. Cassie's look is a dart that says *not a word!*

On his way to the bathroom Bennett finds the thermostat and cranks up the AC. He splashes cold water on his face, then calls Margot. Just the way she says his name is a comfort. He tells her, "I'm in Twilight Zone Hell with Jesus and Kenny G." He loves her laugh. He tells her how uptight Cassie is. "She's going to fight me on this."

"Bennett," Margot says. "You need time with your father, alone, to talk things out. You need to make this happen if you're ever going to move on." Margot thinks he and his dad need to talk about that time, about what happened, how he blames himself.

"I know," he says. "You're right."

"How is your dad?" Margot asks.

"I don't know. Cassie has him locked in his room."

Margot sighs, says she has to go.

The upstairs hallway is wide and silent, the carpet plush. He taps on the last door, open a crack. Dad's lying on his bed, head in hands, staring at the ceiling. Nine months before, when Bennett flew out to watch the Super Bowl, he was fine. They talk almost every week. Cassie thinks she needs to protect Dad. She talks about dementia, but she'll say anything to keep Dad under her control. Still, Bennett steels himself for a shock.

"Dad?"

"Bennett!" Dad sits up and puts on his glasses. His white hair is slicked back, his shirt crisp. Bennett strides to meet him, hand outstretched. Dad stands, opens his arms. Bennett steps into his Old Spice embrace but they are men who shake. "I'm so glad you're here!" Dad says. A smudge makes a rainbow across one of his lenses. "You're getting taller." He makes a face. "I'm shrinking."

"No. You look good, Dad."

By seventeen, Bennett was two inches taller than his father; now he towers over him. Dad pulls on a turkey cardigan. Bennett groans. Founding partner of his firm, he practiced corporate law for forty years, always well dressed, an elegant man. He's missed a spot shaving, and the triangle of white whiskers by his left ear brings a lump to Bennett's throat.

"How's New York?"

"It's great!" Bennett says too loudly. "The colors were amazing this year." He sounds like a goddamn real estate agent.

"I miss it," Dad says. Bennett wonders if "it" includes Mom.

"We'll have a great New York Christmas." Bennett elbows his arm. "I got 'Risk'!"

"Oh!" Dad points at the clock beside his bed. "We're missing kickoff."

Lily pokes her head in. "Grampa?"

"Princess!"

She runs to him. "I had to watch a movie 'cuz I'm loud."

"We got in trouble for playing piano," Bennett says. "But this girl has talent!"

Dad hugs Lily close. He wasn't an affectionate father. They went to ballgames, played 'Risk', poker for pretzel sticks, but they never talked about feelings. Never talked about Mom. Dad got her specialists, treatment, but she always went off her meds. He loved her brand of crazy until he didn't. When Bennett was twelve his dad left the marriage for his office and Bennett to man the loony bin. Three years later, on Thanksgiving, she got creative with rope; hung herself from the staircase banister. Margot tells Bennett it's not his fault, but Bennett never heard that from his dad. Or Cassie.

Lily looks between them, her brow wrinkled. "Are you going with Uncle Bennett?"

"Of course," Dad says.

"Why?"

"The game's starting," Dad says.

Confused, Lily puts her hands on her hips.

"Uh-oh." Bennett lays his palm on Lily's forehead and feigns concern. "She's got it, Dad."

"Yep," he says.

"What?" she asks, head swinging between them.

"Football fever," they say in unison. Lily beams.

Jason's man cave is loud with pregame hype. The décor is half Wild West, half medieval: a suit of armor guards the bar. Margot would think it's funny too, but she'd flash a sly smile with those dimples that knocked him out the moment they met. She'd tell Bennett to behave. He texts a selfie with the metal suit, arm flexed: *Men of Steel.*

Dad sits in a large leather chair looking like a cactus in a too big pot. Lily climbs into his lap. He pats Bennett's hand and asks for a scotch.

"Two-fisted drinker?" Jason asks as Bennett pours the drinks at the bar.

"One's for Dad."

Jason raises his eyebrows. "He's not supposed to drink."

Worry wobbles through Bennett. "Since when?"

Dad shouts, "Kickoff!" and accepts a faux beer from Peewee without complaint. Bennett pours the second scotch into his own and sits on the arm of Dad's chair. Lily pats his knee.

"Touchdown!" Dad says, and high-fives everyone.

"We're Jets fans," Bennett reminds him, then stands and retraces his steps to the AC control and cranks it back up.

"What are you doing?" Cassie rushes down the hall, turkey baster in hand.

"It's sweltering!" he says.

"Take off your jacket."

He grabs her elbow. "Cassie, Dad's coming to New York."

She sighs wearily. "It's not a good idea. "

"Nothing bad's gonna happen," he says. She just gives him a weary smile, shakes her head, and turns up the heat.

Watching the game reminds Bennett of a division playoff, years ago, fourth quarter, he and Dad on the edge of their seats, Mom out shopping. The phone rang. Dad motioned for Bennett to answer. A cop with a Jersey accent asked for his father. Dad yelled, "They're going for it on fourth!" The cop said, *Hello? Are ya there?* "Wrong number," Bennett said, and hung up.

Halfway through the second quarter, Dad's asleep. Bennett finds the women busy in the kitchen and offers help. They stop talking. Ashley blushes. Cassie averts her eyes. Okay then. He wanders into the dining room, rearranges the placeholder turkeys to put Dad and Lily beside him.

Outside, the sunlight's a shock. It's raining in New York. He lies across a hammock, his glass on his chest, staring into the white sky. "I'm on the fucking moon," he tells the Seuss-like cactus beside him, then remembers hearing about a cactus exploding with tarantulas in someone's apartment. Urban legend or not, he sits by the pool. Margot's words, *if you're ever going to move on*, buzz inside him. She texted a response to his metal man photo: *Tough guys!* He calls. No answer. Lily clomps across the patio and stands before him, hands on hips.

"I don't want Grampa to go."

"It's only a visit."

"He'll forget me."

"No way. You're unforgettable."

Lily gives him a doubtful look then walks over to the pool edged in stone and climbs onto the diving board. Cassie moved their father across the country to this desert world. But next month Bennett's bringing him home for Christmas. Lily bounces on the diving board over the deep end, an accident about to happen.

Beyond her, thousands of birds burst into the air in a black cloud, reassemble into a dark line, sunlight flashing wing to wing as they soar, swooping, a wave, pulsing in and out. He wonders how they know when to turn. His breath surges in his chest, his fingers tap out their rhythm. He wants to show Margot but remembers he's alone. Delight turns to ache. He takes out his phone, films the swallows in flight, texts: *Wish u were here.*

"Push me!" Lily says and climbs into the swing on the AstroTurf lawn. Bennett pushes her, with one hand, careful of his drink, tormenting himself with thoughts of Margot moving on with someone else.

"Not like that!" Lily says.

"Geez, does your mom give you bossy lessons?"

"Geez is making fun of Jesus."

"So, report me to the Jesus police," he says. "I'm sure there's some inside."

As everyone heads to the dining room Bennett exchanges Kenny G for Scofield, a CD he gave them last Christmas, still sealed in cellophane. He pulls out Dad's chair, helps Lily into hers.

"Dad?" Cassie pats the chair beside her. She frowns as everyone sits in the wrong places.

Jason bows his head. "Thank you, Lord, ..." Cassie's eyes are closed, hands braided tight, fingertips red. She used to be agnostic. Bennett drains his scotch during the Amen chorus. Dad winks, there's nothing wrong with him. Whenever his mother was away "for a rest," Bennett pretended it was just the two of them, father and son against the world.

Plates become mountains of turkey and stuffing, cranberries, yams, and the eating begins. The bald lawyer tells a story about one of his clients, a defensive tackle caught being stupid in public. Bennett cuts Lily's turkey and tells Dad about his new apartment, near Central Park, full of light.

"Sounds expensive," Dad says, drowning his stuffing in gravy.

Bennett explains it's rent-controlled, he's subletting from a friend working in Vienna for two years. "Margot helped fix up your room."

"I like her!" Dad sets his fork down, interrupts the talk. "Bennett has a wonderful girl."

"We've covered that," Bennett says, avoiding Cassie's knowing look.

Dad sips his wine, clicks Bennett's glass. Lily clicks too, spilling juice, turning Bennett's turkey red. He pretends to switch plates, making her laugh.

"No wine for Dad!" Cassie says.

"Just a celebratory inch."

"Well, that's it!"

Bennett salutes her. She purses her lips. He used to make her laugh. Peewee compliments Jason on the wine and Lily delights Bennett with a convoluted story about her classmate "Stinky Max." Talk turns to education.

"Dad?" Cassie says, pointing to the bald guy. "Marty asked you about schools."

"Jesus, Cassie," Bennett says. "You don't have to translate."

"I don't think your father heard," Marty's big wife says. She speaks! Her voice is tight and high. Marty asks again what's wrong with education, though it's clear he has the answer.

"In my day," Dad says, "kids did as they were told. Or else." He makes a fist. Bennett laughs. He never laid a hand on Bennett, who cut school plenty. "Mothers stayed home and took care of the kids."

Cassie's look says, *See?* Bennett never brought anyone home because his mother was there, until that one Sunday. He was with friends, including a girl—his heart-hammering crush. He needed money. His mother had been "better," so he took a chance. They found her in the kitchen on a stool in a negligee and red heels, drinking gin, writing notes she taped to cabinets. He raced to his room for his wallet and came back to find her dancing, showing her breasts. He pushed his friends outside, went back, and yelled at her, "Take the damn pills!" He stayed with friends, didn't go home until the following Thursday. Thanksgiving. Cassie and Dad were at the kitchen table. Dad looked flattened, eyes unfocused, a face that haunts Bennett still. "Where were you?" Cassie cried. "You left Mom alone?" She'd hanged herself that morning. Dad never said a word, not then, not since. Afterwards, Cassie quit painting, got an MBA, met Jason, found religion in Arizona, and turned into someone else.

"Cassandra," Ashley drawls, "this turkey's so moist." Peewee, mouth full, mumbles agreement. "Is this your music, Bennett?" Ashley twists a strand of her streaked hair. "Peewee says you're a jaaazz musician." She giggles.

"Bennett plays piano, guitar, and trumpet," Dad says, ticking off on his fingers. Bennett puffs with his pride, then feels like an ass. "He's in a band." Dad looks uncertain.

"Yep. You'll see us play next month."

"Every night?" Cassie asks, then disappears into the living room.

Ashley laughs nervously, her cheeks pink with wine.

"Will you play again, later?" Peewee asks. The Scofield stops, Kenny G returns, then Cassie.

"I guess not," Bennett says.

Jason circles the table refilling glasses. He whispers to Cassie, who nods and gulps her wine.

"I've never been to Manhattan," Ashley says.

"The city's beautiful in the snow!" Dad leans in, eyes bright. "There's skating in Central Park."

"Dad's spending Christmas with me," Bennett explains. "In my new place, by the park."

"A bachelor pad, eh?" Peewee says with a wink.

Dad's chuckles. "That's right."

"I got Jets tickets," Bennett says, remembering their thrill of anticipation as the subway doors opened at the stadium stop before a game.

Lily pokes Bennett's arm. "Can I go?"

"What do you say, Dad? Shall we bring a princess?"

"Enough!" Cassie says. "Everyone's happy the way things are."

"You are. My sister used to love New York," Bennett tells the table. "A real bohemian. Threw wild parties."

Marty looks at Cassie like he's uncertain about her now.

"That was a lifetime ago," Cassie says.

"Now she's a born-again Pilgrim."

"Hey. Be nice to big sis," Peewee says, looking warily from Bennett to Cassie.

"New York," Cassie says, pointing with her fork, "is not a healthy place."

"Is it New York's fault?" Bennett asks. "Or just mine?" Silence. Lily pats his arm with concern.

Cassie tells her friends, "It's sweet he wants Dad to visit, but he can't take care of him."

"Cassie," Jason cautions, raking his fingers through his hair.

"He's not a child," Bennett counters. "Last time you said, 'It's too hot, you're out every night,' like I'm some asshole."

Everyone freezes. Dad stares at his plate.

"You sweared," Lily whispers.

"Okay." Jason pushes his chair back, pats his flat belly. "That was delicious, Cassandra. Let's take a break before dessert." He gives Bennett a warning look. Peewee says the game's back on. Everyone scatters, the women ferry dishes to the kitchen. Bennett helps his father up.

"Take a walk, Dad?"

Dad turns, brow creased, as if it's a confusing question. He grips Bennett's shoulder. Bennett tenses.

"The game's on," Dad says and follows the men to the cave.

Bennett drops back into his chair. When he was young, he tried talking to his dad about what happened, but he always put Bennett off with, "We'll talk tomorrow." Cassie urged him to leave it alone. But

Margot's right, they need to talk it all out. While they still can. He's desperate for a smoke. He pours himself another scotch, adds ice; it's a desert out there.

The driveway is steeper as it descends, harder to negotiate. He feels the alcohol heavy in his legs and tries to count his drinks but his brain's busy battling Cassie and what she'll say next to keep Dad to herself. He smacks his head getting into the rental car and curses.

Lily bangs on the window. Bennett's heart flips.

"Jesus, you scared the shit out of me."

"You swear," Lily says. Her dress is MIA. She's made a turban of her undershirt.

"Yeah? Well, you walk around half-naked."

She screws up her face. "You're talking funny."

"And you're supposed to keep your dress on."

She blows a raspberry. "I'm a indigenous peoples."

"Good. Hold my glass." He gets out of his car, throws his jacket over the seat, and lights up, hands shaking. Lily sniffs his drink, takes a sip. "Hey!"

She coughs, sputters, her eyes tear.

"That's what you get for stealing booze."

She sheepishly hands him the glass, then her eyes widen. "You. Are. Smoking!"

"It's my peace pipe."

"Can I do it?"

"No. Your mother would scalp me."

"'Cuz she's your big sister?" Lily asks, delighted.

"Exactly."

She considers this, then asks quietly, "Is that why you fight her?"

He wants to ask what she's heard. "It's complicated." He sets off walking past tile-roofed McMansions each with cactus, a rock garden, and a pole sporting a limp flag. Lily follows.

"Is that why you're taking Grampa away?"

"It's just a visit."

"I know. I'm coming too!" She takes his hand and skips beside him, then squats, scoops soil in her hands, tries to spit but dribbles on her chin. He shows her how it's done, depositing a glob in the dirt. "Nice! Do it again."

"No, that's gross." He flicks ice cubes from his glass, some scotch. "There. A sacrifice to art."

"It's war paint," Lily says, mixing a muddy paste. She draws lines on her face and chest, then spins in circles, wobbly in red boots, mirroring his insides, chanting, "I'm going to New Yo-ork." Her tights sag at the crotch, her turban slips over her eyes. Her laughter is the best music all day. God, he'd love to have kids. With Margot. She'd be the best mother but it's just too risky. He once asked Cassie if she worried about Lily, but she refused to discuss it.

"Chase me!" Lily says, running, giggling, looking back at him until she trips. He kneels and brushes dirt from her hands and knees. "It didn't bleed," she says, so brave.

A car pulls up with a blast of air that knocks Bennett over. A cop gets out and looks down from behind dark glasses. Bennett struggles to his feet, tries to help Lily up, but she shakes her head, frightened. The cop raises her sunglasses revealing bright blue eye shadow.

"War paint's big in Arizona," he tells Lily. The unsmiling cop straightens her hat, pats her gun. Her name tag reads: Officer Mace. Bennett throws his head back, laughs and staggers. "Nice aptronym."

She squints, eyes his unruly hair, his black clothes.

"A name that matches an occupation?"

Her partner, a black man with a short Afro, climbs out too. Officer Dickson. Mace takes Bennett's glass, sniffs.

"Alcohol." She holds it out to Dickson.

"Eighteen-year-old scotch," Bennett says. "Have a nip. We won't tell."

"Let's see some ID," Mace says.

Bennett pats his pockets. "Damn," he says. "My birth certificate's home with my turkey sweater." This makes him laugh harder. The smart man in his brain is telling him to shut the fuck up, but he has a long head start on pissed off. He holds up his right hand. "I'm a citizen. I swear."

"Intoxicated?"

Bennett considers this. "Maybe. Why? Has Arizona outlawed that too?"

Dickson's the good cop. "Eighteen-year-old scotch, eh? Someone's enjoying himself."

"Well, the scotch is good." Bennett wrinkles his nose. "Family."

Dickson nods like he understands.

"Is this your little girl?" Mace asks.

"My sister's."

"Where's your sister?"

"At home, overdoing Thanksgiving."

"What's her name?"

"Cassie."

"Public intoxication is illegal. I could arrest you," Mace says.

"Why? No Mexicans to torment?"

Dickson lowers his brow. Mace leans over Lily, whose lower lip trembles.

"You're scaring her," Bennett says. "It's okay, Lily."

"You said her name's Cassie."

"No. Cassie's my sister."

"What's your name?" Mace asks Lily, who glares, lips pinched tight, reminding Bennett of his mother flipping off cops.

"Atta girl," he says and wonders if this is something he's inherited: ramping things up when they're coming apart.

Mace sniffs. "Did he give you alcohol?"

Lily nods. "He gived it to me for war paint. I couldn't make spit."

"Gave," Mace corrects.

"Don't edit her. She's an improvisationalist." Bennett slips on the esses. It takes him three tries to say it right. "And a indigenous peoples."

Mace asks again for his ID.

"I told you. I'm legal. Third-generation New Yorker."

Mace smirks. Dickson motions her over, says something about Thanksgiving. They argue and it's clear Mace is out for blood. Bennett reaches into his pocket for a cigarette and she lunges, pins him to the car. That's when Lily starts to cry.

Jason's jaw drops to see his little girl between two cops at the door. He picks Lily up and confirms that Bennett is his brother-in-law, a fact he doesn't look happy about. Tears streak Lily's war paint, proof that Bennett has a knack for hurting women. Cassie watches at the window, stricken. Peewee steps outside, the cops recognize the football star and forget about Bennett, thrilled to reminisce about past games and get autographs. Lily gives Jason a blow-by-blow, clearing Bennett, explaining her war paint. Jason's mouth twitches with what Bennett hopes is amusement.

"Oh, shit," Bennett says. "Go ahead, laugh."

"You sweared again!" Lily says and reaches for him. He takes the war-painted bundle of her in his arms, undone by her easy forgiveness.

Ten minutes later, Cassie stomps into the dining room with a bowl of whipped cream, announces dessert like it's punishment, then slices a pumpkin pie to pieces. Everyone sits. Bennett thanks Peewee, who winks, unsmiling. Jason sets coffee before Bennett. There's no music now.

"They wanted my birth certificate. I don't even look Mexican," Bennett says. No one laughs.

"Elaine made this pie." Cassie indicates the big brunette and slaps whipped cream on a slice. "Perhaps you could shut up so we can enjoy it?"

"Mommy," Lily whispers. "Shut up's bad."

"That's right," Bennett says. Cassie extends a plate held high on her palm. Bennett declines.

"Cassandra," Jason warns. She sets it down and eats with determination.

The big brunette strokes her baby's cheek, smiling with naked love. Free of the tense work of glaring at Bennett, her face is tender, reminding him of another face—his mother's?— when he'd come home crying after a scrape with a boy who hurt him with "sticks, stones, and words," he'd said as she kissed his cheeks. He closes his eyes, wondering if he's imagining it, Chopin on the turntable, a surging sonata like a joyful physical presence in the room that played as she held him, whispering a tale of a boy and his mother searching for a magical music box. Margot says he should focus on good memories of his mother instead of beating himself up for what happened, but he's always insisted he has none.

"Wake up, Uncle Bennett," Lily whispers, patting his arm. Bennett opens his eyes.

They're all gone now. Dad's on the sofa reading the paper. Bennett, head pounding, sits beside him, his longing physical, pathetic.

Dad lowers his paper. "I'm glad you're here!"

"Yeah, but you almost had to bail me out of jail this time."

Dad's tilts his head, looks confused.

"Don't you miss New York? I do, and I've only been gone a day." It's Margot he misses. Bennett wants to ask: Can we talk about it? Just blurt it out: Do you blame me? but Cassie sits down on Dad's other side.

"I'm tired," Dad says, folding his paper.

"He's tired," Cassie echoes. She looks exhausted.

"We're all tired," Bennett says, "but I'm leaving tomorrow."

Dad stands. "I think I'll say goodnight."

"But we need to figure this out!" Bennett says.

"Let's talk tomorrow."

Tomorrow! The word explodes in Bennett's head. He follows his father into the foyer. "Tomorrow, Dad?" He grabs his arm. "When is that? I need to know."

Dad shrinks back, rummages in the closet, and pulls out his coat. "Hope it's not snowing."

"Dad?"

"Thank your wife for dinner." He hugs Bennett and opens the front door.

"Dad." Cassie swoops in. "You're home."

"Oh, look!" Dad says, pointing out at the night.

Bennett stands between them, gaping up at a sky making a spectacle of itself. A riotous swirl of reds and golds. His father clutches his hand. It's terrifying.

Cassie gives Bennett a look so freighted with sorrow he's unable to do anything but watch when she leads Dad back inside and up the stairs, just as she did so many times with Mom when she'd had too much or was too much. And he understands; it wasn't just Dad she worked so hard to keep to herself.

He checks his phone. No calls. He takes a picture of the crazy sunset and searches for words to text. Words to make things right.

Patch of Grass

Rick yells over the wind as they walk, a convoluted story involving software copyrights, work that kept him at his office until two a.m. Michele feigns interest, but like the wind, her mind bats at his words. The kids race ahead, skirting trash bins, scuffing their light-up shoes through crisp plate-sized brown leaves that cartwheel down the sidewalk and gather in the gutter. Michele extends her palm to the darkening sky and finds the first raindrops. She longs for thunder and lightning.

They make it into Kaffeine's, their neighborhood coffee shop, as it begins to pour. Rick stands in line to order their drinks. The tables are all full, so Michele waits against the dark wooden cabinets filled with mugs, flyers, and teas. Tommy and Amber excitedly point out their mailman, sipping a tall cup of coffee. He's the only carrier who delivers the right letters to the right houses before noon. Michele waves when he leaves. He is always crisp and quick with a smile. He once told Michele he loved his job, that all he ever wanted was to be a mailman. She is awed by such certainty.

She's relieved to recognize no one else but the dozen faces of genius framed on the walls, people who changed the world by challenging the predictable: Einstein and his made-for-madness hair, Hendrix, Gandhi, Kahlo, Wilde. Amber grips her sweatshirt. Michele fingers her daughter's crazy hair, sticking up on one side after she styled it with scissors "all by myself."

Outside, the rain comes down so hard it blurs the world. A man peers in between cupped hands, rain pouring down his black trench coat and the black hair falling into his face. His breath steams the glass. He searches the shop until his eyes meet Michele's and his face breaks into a smile of dark empty spaces. Thrilled at being seen, he rushes to the door, slips in like a shadow, eyes fixed on Michele. The neighborhood crowd inches in discreet measure north, south, and east of him as he moves like an arrow to her.

"Hello," he says, his voice scratchy. He steps close. The smell of his wet wool competes with the aroma of roasted coffee beans from warmer regions of the world. His eyes are wide, blue, and filled with unsaid things. They would look demonic but for the long black lashes that fringe them. He holds out his hand to her, a gesture part dare, part desperation. Amber tugs on her sweatshirt. Tommy stares at the man's camouflage pants.

Michele takes a step back. They are the same height. Rick drums on the counter, his back to her as the strange man stares.

"Would you like some coffee?"

He whips his head back and forth, spraying rain, and thrusts his hand at her again. Michele hesitates, then takes it. He holds her hand gently in his, rough and solid cold. He shakes it slowly, up and down. A shiver runs down her arm, and his eyes widen, his smile broadens. The children smile too, their upturned faces moving between them. The man standing next to Michele expands protectively, for her sake or his own she can't tell.

"Hell-O," the ragged man says. "Hell-O." As if he's a stranger to the language. He rocks on his feet, narrows one eye, and whispers, "I didn't forget you."

"Okay." Michele tries to pull her hand free. He doesn't let go. She is aware of people watching, happy not to be her, a woman who invites the unwanted.

"Hey!" Rick shouts, his face alert with alarm as he moves toward them, the kids' drinks topped with whipped cream held high. The man reluctantly drops her hand and cuts a ragged seam through the throng. His wet coat flaps against people who lurch out of his way, and then he's gone, into the rain.

She looks down at her hand, surprised not to see something fetid, something foreign. Behind the counter, Rachel the barista calls Michele by her order, "double cap," not by name. She has purple and black braids, and her eyelids are shadowed a vivid green. The silver bob piercing her tongue winks as she mouths, wanna wash your hands? Michele slips her hand in her pocket, pretending she doesn't understand, and follows Rick to stools in the front of the shop, at the large window to the street.

Rick gives Michele her drink, eyebrows raised. She takes it in her left hand, feeling the pleasure of doing just this small thing in an unfamiliar way. She smiles into her cup. Rick pushes her hair from her face. She needs a haircut. He thinks she's letting herself go.

"What was all that about?" he asks.

"He said—"

"What?"

"Nothing." She shakes her head. Rick squeezes her shoulder. "He thought he knew me."

"Freak," Rick says. "I can't believe you shook his hand."

She shrugs. "I couldn't just pretend he wasn't there, that he didn't exist."

Rick cocks his head like he's having difficulty hearing.

"You know what I mean."

Rick's face rumples with concern; he squints, making up his mind about her.

"He thought he knew me," she repeats. She wants him to understand, but he won't even try. She sips her coffee while her right hand hides a secret taboo in the soft pocket of her sweatshirt. Someone turns up the interior lights. She blinks, startled by her reflection in the window; she looks overexposed, like a ghost.

"You're shivering," he says, and offers his coat.

"Am I?"

He starts to speak, then sighs, unfolds his newspaper to the sports page, and reads to Tommy about the upcoming playoff game.

"Rick!" a voice booms behind them. It's a chunky redheaded guy in a jogging suit, one of Rick's partners. A woman in an identical outfit hangs on his arm. He claps Rick on the back.

"Great Scott!" Rick's voice is fake-friendly. He stands, towering over Scott. He knows she can't stand him but says, "You remember my wife? Michele?"

"Of course," Scott says with a proprietary smile. He swaggers even when he's standing still. "How could I forget?"

Michele never told Rick about Scott's drunken move on her at the firm's last Christmas party. She'd escaped the mind-numbing shoptalk to see the city lights from the deck. Scott snuck up behind her and clapped his arms around her waist, stumbling against a potted cypress as he pressed his hard-on against her, licking her neck. She stomped her stiletto heel into his foot. "Jesus!" he'd yelled, rubbing his shoe, staring at her like she was crazy. Inside, Rick was talking to the founding partner. She sidled up to him, wanting to tell him, but he brushed her off, suggested she join the other wives, so she kept it to herself.

Scott thrusts his hand at her, and for an awkward moment she doesn't move. Rick shifts uncomfortably. Michele looks into Scott's smug round face and gives him a smile to match the weather. She pulls her hand from her pocket, imagining his face if he knew who'd held it last. She squeezes, extra hard.

"Whoa. Your wife has one hell of a grip!" Scott tells Rick, rubbing his hand as if in pain. His voice is annoyingly loud. "This is Cindy." He puffs out his chest. "She's a hot new analyst." Cindy smiles up at him adoringly. Rick frowns.

Michele tries not to laugh as she shakes Cindy's hand too.

Cindy asks Michele what she does. Her deep voice is a surprise. Before Michele can answer, Rick, clearly pleased with himself, says, "She has the hardest job of us all. She's staying home and raising our kids."

Michele grits her teeth.

Cindy flashes a too-wide smile. "Oh, yeah? That's so great!" She reminds Michele of Amber's Barbie, but when she sees the way Scott grips her arm, she feels a pang of sorrow for the woman. She wants to yell, *Run! Now!* Rick works his jaw as he listens to Scott brag about his department's success.

"It's Saturday. No shoptalk," Michele says, and is rewarded with Rick's original smile, the one she rarely sees.

"We're going to the gym. Just revving up," Scott says, hoisting his coffee and taking a noisy slurp. "What are you kids up to?"

"There's a Dorothea Lange retrospective," Michele says, "at the—"

"And the Seahawks game." Rick talks over her, elbowing Tommy.

"—at the SAM," Michele finishes, and turns to the children, a necessary diversion. They are ogling a red fire truck.

Amber claps. "Look, Daddy! It's the fire truck Miss Jennifer took us to see." When he doesn't respond, she says, "Daddy!"

"Miss Jennifer?" Rick asks, creasing his brow.

"My teacher, at Happy Trails."

"Oh," Rick says. "Miss Jennifer!" Amber beams.

Scott snorts. "Happy Trails?"

Amber glares at him, fists clenched. "That's my school. Don't laugh at it."

"Good girl," Michele says, smoothing Amber's hair. Scott sputters an apology.

Tommy grabs her arm. "Look, Mommy, your friend."

"Who?"

"That man who shook your hand."

"Where?"

Tommy points his chubby finger until she sees the man talking to a fireman under the awning next door.

"I can't see," Amber whines. Tommy grabs her head and turns it to the man. Michele pulls his hands away and tells him to be gentle. The man turns as if he feels them watching; he leans his head toward them in a sinuous motion. Tommy waggles his head too. Amber, seeing Tommy's not afraid, sticks her tongue out. The man returns the favor, making the kids laugh.

"Look at that freak out there," Scott says.

Rick turns. "He hit on Michele a few minutes ago."

"Oh, how gross!" Cindy shivers and squeezes Scott's arm.

"*He* didn't mean any harm," Michele says, giving Scott a look.

"Watch out, Tommy," Rick says. "Your mother has a bleeding heart!"

Tommy looks at Michele with alarm.

All morning the man's words echo in her head: I didn't forget you. Could he really know her? After lunch, she lies down with Amber so she'll nap but it's Michele who falls asleep. Amber's gone when she wakes.

From the kitchen window Michele sees her family raking leaves; the sun is out and the garden steams. Rick chases the kids, who jump into the soggy piles he's formed. They are soaking wet. She opens the refrigerator and leans on the door. It's full of food but there's nothing she wants. She pads on bare feet across the cold tile floor. In the living room she sits on the carpet before the bookshelves and pulls out her high school yearbooks. She leans against the sofa and flips through the one from freshman year, full of silly inscriptions from people she barely remembers. *Have a great summer! Friends 4 Ever!* I's dotted with hearts. She turns the pages, studying the stony expressions of boys, the coy smiles of girls, the theater geeks, the smokers and jocks, all captured in photos she took. There she is with her camera, wearing her wacky homegrown clothes, in photos surrounded by messages: *To Michele—the craziest girl I know!* She scans the faces for an intense, dark-haired boy. She pulls out the yearbook from her senior year, half her life ago. *Hey crazy chica—have a great life! Bring the Joy! Go Be Amazing!* They believed her bound for great adventure. She turns to her own picture. Michele Johansson. Her hair was short then and bleached white. Her eyes stare out from behind pointy, red-framed glasses she thought were cool. Most of the girls wear pearls or tiny crucifixes around their necks, but she sports the Celtic symbol for joy on a green velvet ribbon. She wonders if she still has it.

The back door slams. Rick tells the kids to take off their shoes and change into dry clothes. The fridge door slaps, a beer hisses. He finds her and sits on the couch, asks what she's doing. She holds up a yearbook. He slides down next to her and offers her his beer. She takes a long drink; the bubbles tickle her nose. Rick points at her picture.

"Is that you?"

Michele nods.

"What a looker." He whistles, draws his finger under her title. "You were voted most unconventional? How'd you earn that?"

"By being myself," she says, lifting her chin.

"Yeah?" He watches her as she turns the pages. "Why this stroll down memory lane?"

She stares at the pictures. "I wondered if that guy went to my high school."

"Should I be worried?" he asks, nudging her with his shoulder. "Is he a flame from your unconventional past?" When she doesn't answer, he smooths her hair, twists a strand in his fingers. "If you want to see that show, go ahead. The kids can watch the game with me." He looks at his watch. "Almost kickoff."

He stands up, grabs the remote. She turns the page. There's a photo of her taking a picture of boys dressed as Jets for 'West Side Story'. She closes the yearbook with a snap and prowls through the cupboard on her knees, delighted to find her old Rollei 35 mm in its box, the camera her grandfather gave her so many years before.

Rick settles on the sofa in front of the TV. The kids pepper him with questions, Tommy about football, Amber about unicorns. They have to ask everything twice. Michele watches them snuggled together, thinking Rick is being a great dad today. She checks the impulse to thank him and wanders through the house tidying up, then out to the garden, where the sun is hesitant. She digs her toes into a damp patch of grass, so green ... She wonders how she can feel so restless and tired at once. The wind whips her hair, which is too long and feels too heavy all the time. She pushes it from her face, rakes her fingers through it, irritated by its weight.

In the bathroom, she peels off her clothes. Working with just the light from the window, she pulls her hair off her neck, takes scissors and cuts, the steel biting through. There's a flutter in her throat as she cuts it even shorter. After rinsing diluted peroxide through what's left of it— one, two, three times—she towels it dry and blows it into spiky curls, her reflection a black-and-white photo. She slides into tight jeans, pulls on the black cashmere turtleneck her mother gave her, and zips up black boots that reach to her knees. She inspects herself in the mirror, thrilled and horrified at her reinvention.

Downstairs, her family is glued to a commercial of beer bottles playing sports. Tommy has his arms behind his head, legs crossed like Rick's, echoing everything his father says. Amber is asleep. Michele fits her boots into the wet, grassy footprints she left on the kitchen floor. She calls goodbye from the door and is gone before they see her. She speeds down their quiet neighborhood street, a freedom flutters in her chest.

The museum is quiet; her bootsteps on the marble floors echo like gunshots off the walls. The Lange exhibit is closed, and the new exhibit isn't up yet. As she passes an exhibit of Impressionists, a Van Gogh catches her eye. She read once that after seeing the work of Impressionists for the first time, he found his own work old-fashioned and dark by comparison and he changed, became a new artist. She stands before his painting, a vibrant, colorful piece called Patch of Grass. The placard beside it says a spectral fluorescence X-ray revealed an older painting beneath. She studies the photo of the original: an unsmiling woman in dark, sorrowful hues. Her eyes say nothing will ever change. Then, two years later, she was buried under grass.

The café at the museum is closed for repairs. She hurries to her car and sits, thrilled by the lightning that finally pierces the clouds. She's too restless to go home. A parking spot across the street from Kaffeine's feels like a gift. She slips into a snug canyon between two monster SUVs, wondering if she'll be able to see her way out.

Inside the line is long. Doesn't anyone have anything better to do? Michele takes her place at the end, her coat dripping. Rachel is still working. The music is loud, Bach concertos for violin and cello, deep and troubling. A man in line complains, "This music's too intense, turn it down," addressing the other barista who has huge gauges in his ears that make Michele shiver.

"Please don't," Michele calls out. "It's perfect."

The chatter in the shop quiets; everyone turns to listen. The man gives her a sour look.

When Michele finally orders, Rachel won't let her pay. "Girl, this music is the only thing that's keeping me sane."

Michele closes her eyes, loving the way the music fits the weather that echoes her mood. Rachel tells her she's working a double shift.

"It's okay," she says when Michele makes sympathetic noises. "I need the cash, but I've had it up to my tits." She makes a chopping motion across her chest and hands Michele her coffee.

"I know what you mean," Michele says. She gestures at the famous faces framed on the wall behind her. "At least you have them."

"Yeah," Rachel says with reverence.

Michele laughs, and maybe it's the music, she asks Rachel for a second coffee, small.

"Love the look, by the way!" Rachel pours, then leans over and touches Michele's spiky hair. Michele touches it too, surprised at what she's done. "Hot date?" Rachel asks.

Michele shakes her head. "Do you ever feel like crawling right out of your own skin?"

"Venus is in retrograde," says a young couple behind her in unison. They have matching hennaed hair, their arms drape across each other's shoulders. They smile, pleased to hold a secret understanding of the mysteries of the world.

"Sounds like trouble," Rachel says, and winks.

Michele leans closer. "I feel like trouble." The force of her words surprises her.

Rachel presses her lips, nods like she understands. Michele pulls her camera from her purse, uncaps the lens, focuses on the diamond stud in Rachel's nose and shoots. Down the line a gray-haired woman complains that she doesn't have forever. When Michele drops a ten-dollar bill in the tip jar Rachel blows a kiss.

Michele's arms and legs thrum with energy as she fits lids on the two cups and takes a seat at the window for the second time that day. She scans the front page of a discarded newspaper with its tales of inhumanity and tosses it aside. She twists sugar packets and jumps when they rip open, spilling on the dark counter. She writes her name in the grainy whiteness, Michele, forming the last e again and again in connecting loops that mean nothing. She thinks of Van Gogh's painting, of science saving art, of how the old and unwanted can be reinvented, colored over. She touches her hair.

People stream in and out, gaggles of teens ordering sugary drinks, a buzz-cut woman with tattoos, a weary-eyed man in a rumpled brown suit, and the ever-present mothers with babies on their backs.

A loud screech of brakes causes a collective inhalation in the shop. It's him, in the middle of the street, crossing against the light. She rushes out the door, her camera bumping her hip, the second coffee in her hand. The sun finds a break in the storm clouds and there is light.

"Hi," she calls, hurrying across the street. He turns at the curb, looks her up and down. She steps onto the sidewalk. Maybe he won't recognize her now.

"Remember me?" she asks. "This is for you." The wind blows her jacket open; the cold makes her nipples hard. She takes a deep breath and extends the coffee, surprised by her nervousness. Sunlight winks on her wedding ring. He stares at her breasts, then finally reaches with both hands to take the cup. He doesn't say a word. His fingers brush hers, icy and shocking. He peels off the cup's plastic lid and glares down at its contents.

"I hope you like it black." She cringes at her apologetic tone.

He pulls a bottle wrapped in a brown paper bag from his pocket, twists it open, and holds it over the cup, upside down, until the last drops fall, fill the cup to the rim. She lifts her camera, focuses, and steals the moment as he raises the cup and slurps.

"Coffee's cold." It's a statement of fact.

"You were late," she says.

He nods his head.

"I wanted to ask you something," she says. He looks at her with those long-lashed eyes. This is not the face she searched for in her yearbooks. "I wanted to ask you what you meant this morning."

He mutters something.

"What?" She bites her thumbnail.

He takes an unsteady step toward her. Fear trills across her shoulders, between her legs. She wants to ask if it was drugs or a conflict of war that made him like this. She imagines a younger, lovelier version of the man.

"You are a weird fucking bitch," he says, his brief smile softening his face.

"Yes," she says. "I am." Her laugh is high pitched.

He howls. Michele jumps.

"Freak," a woman in aviator glasses spits as she hurries past them.

"What do you think?" he says, looking her up and down as if she's stolen something from him and hidden it on her person. "Give me cold coffee, take my picture, and you'll stop being a whore?" He stares at her with those wild blue eyes. As she pulls her coat closed, he drops his pants, thrusts his hips at her. She has to look. His flaccid penis wobbles, a sad, hairless creature. He steps closer. She wants to slam him against the SUV behind him, shock him right back.

"Stop it!" She steps away and thinks of her family, secure in their idea of her, how she'll stop at the market on her way home, anticipate their needs. It's this that frightens her most.

The world of the sidewalk goes about its business as the man turns, exposed, arms raised to the sky. People bend into themselves, hurry by with screwed-up faces, but someone yells that they called the cops. The man opens his mouth, but before he can say anything more, Michele turns, and runs back across the street. An Uber swerves, tires shrieking as it brakes, missing her by inches. The driver blares his horn and yells, "Fucking idiot!" as she races to the other side while the man with his pants down is laughing, screaming, "Crazy bitch!"

The loud *whoop-whoop, whoop-whoop* of a police siren cuts the air. A black-and-white squeals to a stop across the street, where a crowd gathers. Rachel rushes out of Kaffeine's; customers follow holding cups.

"Damn," she says. "You okay?"

"Yeah." Michele paces. "No." She laughs, trying to catch her breath.

The silver stud bobs in Rachel's tongue as she asks, "What happened?"

"I gave him coffee. He pulled down his pants." The words catch in her throat.

Rachel curses, lights a cigarette, takes a deep pull. Michele exhales with her.

Across the street the man sits on the sidewalk. A big policeman stands over him; the other cop talks to people who point at Michele.

She turns her back to it all. In the coffee shop's large plate glass window, the street scene is reflected, red lights flashing, Rachel's large frame beside a narrow woman in black, her white, white hair standing on end. A dark cloud eclipses the sun, and the street scene fades to reveal customers inside, watching.

Finger Food

Davis Latimer sits in his Mustang outside the sushi restaurant he's just left, wondering why he keeps getting it wrong with Nina. Black-and-red Japanese lanterns swing wildly above people rushing by, bent into the wind. A storm is coming. He sighs and puts the key in the ignition of his midlife crisis, as his kids call his car. But hell, it was never his plan to be alone at fifty-four. Thanks a lot, cancer. He'd needed a change and a Mustang seemed a good start.

Sushi wasn't his choice, but his oldest daughter, Claire, insisted he take his youngest to dinner. "Nina needs help. Talk to her, see for yourself!" But talking to Nina is never easy.

When he'd arrived, a woman speaking Japanese tried to steer him to a table. He gestured outside and said—in what his wife called his primitive language—that he was waiting for someone. And there she was, crossing the street, her long frame bent into a fierce wind that tossed her hair, black now, yellow at the ends. She wore a shabby black outfit—tights, short skirt, torn sleeveless top—and carried a huge bag. He didn't get it. She was a cute girl who dressed like a homeless person. But the clothes weren't the worst part. The closer she came the less there was of her, and what was there looked tied up in knots. He should have waited outside instead of worrying that the cold wind would fuck up his thinning hair.

At the glass door her eyes slid up and down her sharp-angled reflection. Davis had the urge to rush to her but was rooted to the burgundy carpet beside an enormous potted palm. She swung the door wide with a clattering of bells. Her face lit up.

"Daddy!"

He felt like a voyeur.

"Hi, kiddo." His legs finally moved, and he met her halfway. She wrestled with her bag while they managed an awkward hug. She was shivering. "Where's your coat?"

"I forgot it," she said, shoulders hunched. He motioned with his finger to indicate lipstick on her teeth. She gave a start. "Oh, thanks." She rubbed it off, bony elbow jutting. "Sorry I'm late. There was no parking."

"No problem." He looked at his watch like he hadn't been counting the minutes, part of him hoping she wouldn't show. "I had a hell of a time myself."

Silver bangles jangled at her wrists as she fluttered her hands, a new tattoo on her arm of a red and orange bird. "I hope you didn't have to park too far away. I forgot how hard it is in this neighborhood. I should have picked—"

"No, no." He waved off her concern. "I'm just across the street." Why was every little thing a problem for her? They hadn't even sat down and he felt irritated. A kimono-clad waitress rushed toward them saying something he couldn't understand. She repeated herself—a string of dissonant syllables—then frowned and turned to Nina.

"We'll just sit at the sushi bar if that's okay." Nina bent her tall, bony body to the woman like she was begging. The waitress led them to the only open seats along the crowded bar. Dave pushed in Nina's chair, next to a young couple entwined in each other's arms, sharing raw fish and whispered conversation. A curvy redhead on his right looked him over.

"Push over, Jackie," the redhead told her friend. "A tall, dark stranger wants to sit beside me."

Nina inhaled sharply and glared at the laughing women, who inched their chairs down. Davis took a deep breath before sitting in the narrow space.

"You look handsome," Nina said, and ran her hand down his sleeve.

"Your mother bought this for me that last Christmas. She had excellent taste." He looked down at the blazer, dreading the day it wore out. "I don't wear it often, it makes me …" He felt foolish talking that way.

"I know. You're saving it." Her eyes were so big. She opened her menu.

"Well, I have a special date tonight," he said.

Her head jerked up. "Who?" She never liked anyone Davis dated.

"My daughter?" Was that relief in her face? The last time he'd introduced Nina to a woman he was seeing, she'd talked only to Davis and reminisced about her mother.

The waitress brought water, bowls of cloudy soup; she asked Davis a question.

"Pardon?"

"Would you like something to drink?" Nina interpreted.

"Sure. Gin and tonic." The waitress shook her head. Nina's brow creased.

"Sorry, Daddy. They only have sake and beer."

"That's hardly your fault," he said. "I'll have what you're having."

"Diet Coke?"

"God, no. Have a drink with me."

She shrugged. "Sake?"

"Two sakes," Davis told the waitress, who looked startled, whirled around silently, and darted to the other end of the bar.

Nina whispered, "Daddy, you don't need to yell."

"Hey, I'm not the one with the language problem here."

Nina sighed. "How's work?"

"Busy. Hired another crew this year. Remember the Matheson boy? He's your age. Started his own construction group. I coached him in Little League, now he's my competition. Makes me feel old."

"He's Lucas's age," she corrected.

He nodded and talked of changes in the construction industry, how young people were slick with computer skills, profiles on Yelp, twittering, things he didn't want to bother with. He'd had some back problems and couldn't do the heavy lifting anymore but didn't want to tell her this. Instead, he rambled on about market projections, knowing he was stalling, wondering how to ask if she was okay. She listened with a vague smile.

"I'm boring you," he said.

"No, you're not." She picked at her soup, extracting tiny white tofu squares she arranged in a circle in a tiny red dish.

The women beside Davis stood to leave. The redhead winked at him. Davis returned her wink with a mock bow. The sushi chef smiled and bowed too, and for a moment Davis relaxed, thinking that this night might turn out okay. Maybe they could talk. When the sushi chef said something unintelligible, Davis shook his head.

"Are you ready to order?" Nina asked.

Davis pointed to menu items with the word grilled in front of them. The chef's white hat banded with Japanese letters put Davis in mind of a rack of lamb, ready for roasting. If only. His girls called him a Neanderthal for his diet of meat and potatoes.

Nina asked the chef for a cucumber roll sliced into eight pieces, rather than six. She lifted her soup bowl and sipped carefully, pinky fingers extended, glancing sidelong at the cooing couple beside her. Davis didn't know if she had a boyfriend but figured it was safer not to ask.

"When's the last time we did this?" he said instead, his voice sounding false.

"My birthday, last February. Remember, it was raining?"

"Right. The Grill."

"You wanted a steak," Nina said.

"Yeah, and you didn't eat."

She tensed. "Yes, I did." Her mouth pursed in and out as she ate her Barbie-doll-sized tofu.

"Maybe some finger food." Now, he told himself. Say something. Are you okay? He'd always enjoyed seeing his girls eat, but as they drifted into their teen years, food became the enemy. Nina had always been the worst, starving herself into Twiggydom. After Claire had her twins, she gained a lot of weight and now he hated to see her eat.

The sushi chef leaned over the glass case and set down wooden trays with pyramids of green paste beside pink ginger; the waitress's sleeve passed between them as she delivered a carafe of hot sake. Nina poured, biting her lower lip.

"Cheers!" Davis lifted his cup. They usually saw each other at Claire's, with the dogs, the husband and tumble of kids, the TV always blaring. He took Nina out every year on her birthday. They talked sometimes on the phone, but it was awkward, especially saying goodbye, not knowing how to hang up but desperate for the call to be over.

"Kampai!" Nina said with a nervous laugh.

She puckered up and sipped like a baby bird. It infuriated him. He wanted to grab the tiny cup out of her hand. He drained his own in one gulp and wondered what the hell his problem was. The chef arranged strips of fish tied to rice on his tray. Nina asked the chef for low-sodium soy sauce and offered some to Davis.

"No, thanks." He refused her dietary quirks.

She watched him eat the first piece.

"Very good," he said, and her shoulders relaxed.

Nina was the baby, Claire the oldest. Lucas was the easy middle one, but he lived in London now for his job. When Lucas had problems, Davis always knew how to help. And he'd taught him things, how to stand his ground, how to keep his best punch ready and when to throw it, how to change a tire, and even how to talk to a girl: Ask them questions, people like to talk about themselves.

"Enough about me," Davis said. "What have you been up to?"

Nina straightened in her chair. "I'm studying choreography and dancing, ballet mostly."

"Is that where you're coming from?"

"No, why?"

He waved a hand over her outfit. She looked down at her crazy clothes.

"I might take a class later, eight-thirty. Jazz. But only if we've finished," she said in a rush, fluttering her hands again.

"I thought you gave up dancing."

"I'm not performing right now, but I still take classes! I can't imagine not dancing!" She'd always been dramatic, something that had tickled him when she was younger.

She'd been a dancer for as long as he could remember. Her mother said she came out of the womb *en pointe*.

The couple next to Nina stood. The young man wrapped a red shawl around his girlfriend's shoulders, their eyes locked as they walked to the door. The chef placed more sushi on Davis's tray as Nina nibbled her cucumber roll.

"How's your work?" Davis asked.

"It's great!" Her face lit up. "Dr. Miller's amazing! I'm learning so much!" She described her work as a research assistant in the biochemistry lab at the college. It had amazed him, her passion for science, because she'd always been a girly-girl. Then he remembered stories he'd heard about professors preying on young female students.

"I hope he behaves himself."

"Dr. Miller is a woman! Just because you don't work with women doesn't mean the world hasn't moved on. And ..." She was off, lecturing him on sexism. Her lips were chapped, her nails bitten down to nubs. Patty always had beautiful hands; he couldn't imagine her ever gnawing on her fingers. And suddenly that longing for Patty rose up inside him. She'd have known just what to say, always good at smoothing things out with the girls. Davis liked to think he was a good father, a good provider, but once the girls hit twelve, they moved to a different country where their bodies changed, where they spoke a private language and became secretive and critical of him. Almost overnight he didn't know the line between interested, annoying, and creepy, so he learned to keep his distance.

"Daddy?"

"What's that?"

"You're a million miles away."

"Just listening," he said. "I'm really glad you like your job."

Nina nodded at the sushi chef, who stood, smiling patiently.

"What else do you want?" Nina asked.

Davis scanned the laminated menu and pointed. The chef barked something at a waitress. Davis picked up the sake carafe, black with orange butterflies. He tried to refill Nina's cup, but she held up a hand.

"I haven't finished what I have."

"It's only a thimbleful," Davis said and topped up her cup. Her chewed fingers fiddled with the ginger. "Are you biting your nails?"

She squeezed her hands together in her lap, shoulders hunched. "Bad habit."

"Your mother got regular manicures. Maybe you could try that."

Her shoulders inched higher.

More sushi had appeared without his noticing.

"Where'd this come from?" He lowered his voice and said to Nina, "Watch out, this guy's sneaky." He laughed.

"Don't be racist."

"What the hell did I say?" he asked, bewildered.

She just shook her head.

"You want anything else?"

"Not yet," she said. "I'm still eating this." She lifted a piece of her cucumber roll expertly with chopsticks.

"I never could get the hang of those. I just eat with my fingers." He grabbed a piece of sushi, stuffed it in his mouth, and set a piece on her tray. "Try this," he said, his mouth full. "It's good." She put it back on his tray.

"Come on, Nina, you've got to eat more than that. Your sister thinks you're starving yourself."

She narrowed her eyes. "Claire? Really?" She pantomimed a large curvy body in the air. "Maybe she's just ..." She looked up at him through lacquered black lashes.

"Jealous? I don't know about that." They were on dangerous territory. "Your mother was always thin."

Nina lifted her chin.

"But not like you. You don't look well." He pointed at her sushi. "Don't you like it?"

"It's great." Her smile was forced, her chin quivered. Shit. The waitress appeared and said something that sounded like machine-gun fire. It was unsettling. Nina's head was all harsh black and yellow. Her natural hair was beautiful, honey colored. Why would she ruin it?

"Do you want some more sake?" she asked.

"Definitely."

Nina whispered to the waitress, who nodded and slipped away. People at the far end of the sushi bar were talking loud, laughing.

"Your hair used to be so thick and shiny." A red-hot worry shot through him.

She smoothed her napkin. "I'm fine." She still had six pieces of sushi on her tray. Her pursed lips reminded Davis of a time when she was two. He was leaving for work. Patty was tending to Lucas's skinned knee. Trying to be a good family man, Davis picked up the bowl of baby mush and offered the spoon to Nina, who closed her lips and swung her head back and forth, rocking her highchair. He tried forcing the spoon into her mouth, but she spit on his suit jacket. "Dammit," he yelled. Patty grabbed the bowl from his hands. "Oh, let me," she said, holding the bowl, kissing Lucas's head, and with her other hand buttering his toast. Claire rushed in to feed Nina, who accepted breakfast from her sister, Daddy deemed not up to the task. He cleaned his jacket with a tea towel. No kisses for him. He left that morning feeling as he had so many times as a father, that he'd failed at something basic. It all came easy to Patty, but couldn't she have helped him? He wondered what she'd really thought of him. Had she complained to her friends? My husband can't even figure out how to feed his own damn kids! Did she play the injured party? Would it have been so hard to say, Like this, try this? He used to comfort himself that maybe she saw it as manly but he'd always wondered if deep down, she'd found him profoundly inept. He wondered what kind of mother Nina would be. If she'd ever have kids. If she'd be a patient wife.

He downed his sake. "Men don't like women too skinny."

As soon as the words left his mouth, he wanted to smack himself. The look on that little-girl face, well, she was twenty-four, but with her skinny arms and raccoon hair, her chapped lips and enormous green eyes, she looked like a poster child. He'd fallen in love with that face the first moment he saw her, even more than with his other two. She'd been Daddy's little girl until puberty changed her allegiance.

"I'm eating!" She popped a piece of cucumber roll into her mouth and chewed and chewed like a ruminant cow. Her nose turned red. Shit.

"I'm sorry. I didn't mean it like that."

Her nose grew redder, her eyes teary. She swallowed. "You think no one could love me."

The waitress returned with another sake and a Diet Coke. When she opened the Coke, it sputtered and foamed as she poured, the ice sizzled and cracked.

"That's not true. Any guy would be lucky to have you."

Nina blew her nose in the flimsy paper napkin. "Did Claire make you ask me out?"

Davis pulled a handkerchief from his pocket and gave it to her. She smoothed it under her hand, ran her finger along the monogram.

"Mom taught me to iron on these. I tried to get them perfect. Line the edges up just right. Did you ever notice?"

"What, that I had nice handkerchiefs? Sure."

"No, did you notice that I did them after Mom got sick?"

How was he supposed to remember the ironing? He'd been a wreck. "Sure."

Her green eyes were fierce as she asked in a shaky voice, "So? Did Ms. Perfect Matronette make you ask me out?"

"She's concerned, but I wanted to see you."

Nina stared through the fogged glass at the pale slabs of fish. "You know, I thought it was strange when you called. Middle of game three? The World Series?" She smirked. "Claire probably planted herself in front of your TV until you called."

"Hey, since when ... I mean ... does a father need an excuse?"

Her eyes grew bright, her breathing fast. "Bathroom," she said, pushed her chair back and hurried across the restaurant. The chair teetered and crashed to the floor, spilling the contents of her purse everywhere: a cell phone, an exercise band, gum, notebook, ridiculous red sunglasses, ballet slippers, a prescription bottle, keys, pens, crumpled Kleenex, makeup, loose change, and more. He palmed the prescription bottle, checking first to see if anyone was watching; a woman's purse was sacred territory. The waitress whispered over and helped him gather the rest. He hung the bag over Nina's chair and read the prescription label: Adderall. He slipped it into his blazer pocket. A small photo album lay on the floor.

He opened it to a picture of Patty before she got sick. Her green eyes stared out at him from the faraway place she'd inhabited sometimes. He longed for her advice, then realized she'd probably tell him to leave it alone, that he'd only make it worse. Somehow the children became her domain; he'd felt they formed a separate clan apart from him. When Lucas began to defy him, challenging him as a man, he'd joined his sisters in making fun of Davis. How had that happened? There was a time when his kids couldn't get enough of him. If Nina had a nightmare, it was his side of the bed, his arms she nestled into, and when he hugged her little body and whispered she was safe, he could take her fear away. If Patty tried to comfort her, Nina screamed, "No! I need Daddy."

Davis couldn't remember the last time he'd done anything but piss her off or make her cry. He flipped through the album to a picture of dancers with Nina in the middle, smiling big. Most of the photos were of people he'd never met. But there was one of all five of them, a family intact, on a long-ago trip to Disneyland, Patty smiling, her head on Davis's chest, his arm around her. In the next one, he's holding Nina's hand and she's beaming up at him. Happy. He looked so young and serious, she was so adorable, so tiny, so sweet.

Nina returned, head down. He took in her thin arms and shoulders, her ridiculous shoes and long legs, skinny, like the seven-year-old's in the photo. He stood and pulled out her chair.

"Thanks," she mumbled as he pushed her in. "Daddy, I'm sorry, I—"

"There's nothing to be sorry about." He lifted her Coke and his sake cup. "Let's drink to our health." He sipped the sake, searching for better words. "Look, I don't know what's going on. I'd like to help but ... clearly, I don't know how."

She stared down at the ice melting in her glass and started to speak but saw the photo album.

"Your purse fell. Everything spilled out. The waitress helped me pick it all up. I looked at your pictures. I hope you don't mind."

"It's okay."

"Can you just try to tell me?" She didn't respond. He put a hand on her tight shoulder. "I'm worried," he said. "You're so thin again, you seem so tense." When she still didn't speak, Davis picked up the photo book and flipped through it, stopping at the picture of the two of them. "Remember this? Your first day of school after we moved here."

She leaned closer. "I was scared. Lucas told me new kids got spanked."

Davis snorted. "Rascal. Your mother was in Florida helping Grandma Ellie after she broke her hip. She hated not being there for you."

Nina ran her finger over the photo. "I loved that dress."

"I walked you to school," he said.

"You were all dressed up. And I had new shoes and socks with ruffled tops."

"You looked like an angel."

For a second, he saw his baby girl. They both looked at the photo.

"I was so scared," she said again.

Me too, he thinks. He took a deep breath. "It must have been hard not having Mom."

She tapped the photo, her eyes far away. "No. I was happy it was you. Why do you think I kept it?" Her lips formed a crooked smile. "You told me I'd love second grade, that lots of things in life are scary and I had to learn to stand toe-to-toe with them."

"Well ... that doesn't sound helpful. Your mother would have known what to say." The deep, throaty laugh from Nina's skinny frame surprised him. Patty's laugh.

"No. She would have said, 'Oh, there's nothing to be afraid of, stop being silly.'" Nina mimicked her perfectly. "She'd have clucked her tongue and fussed over my dress."

"Really?"

"Yes. You told me if anyone was mean you'd punch their father in the nose. I loved that."

He couldn't imagine himself ever saying that.

"Don't you remember? We laughed all the way to school."

"I just remember how scared you were and how hard it was to leave you there."

She arranged her cups and dishes in a line in front of her. "I still am."

"What?"

"Scared." She fiddled with her chopsticks.

"Yeah," he said. She still hadn't finished her cucumber roll. The waitress appeared.

"Tea?" she asked. It was the first word she'd said that he understood. They watched in silence as she filled their cups. Nina lifted her thin face to Davis. She was a mystery; the way Patty could be.

"You're like her, you know," he said.

"No way."

"Yes. Granted, you look like she did before she— when she was sick—and that scares the hell out of me. But you've got her smile, her laugh, her big eyes, and her damned hard-headedness. And so much shit in your purse!"

Nina gave him a watery smile.

They walked in silence to her car, her big purse bumping between them. He said he'd call soon to get together.

"If you want to talk," he said. "I'm here for you."

"I know."

He hugged her, feeling her ribs in his arms, afraid he'd hurt her. Don't you disappear on me too. She was so quiet he wondered if he'd said it out loud.

He tells himself it's time to go, but he just sits in his Mustang across from the restaurant, in no hurry to return to his empty house. People keep pulling up beside him, waving to ask if he's leaving. He waves them off and imagines Nina at her jazz class telling the other dancers, "Ugh, I had to have dinner with my father." All of them trading knowing looks about wasting time. He wonders when he became such a coward.

Looking up through the sunroof to a blurred field of stars, he wishes for a do-over, wishes he'd confronted her about the pills. Is it serious? An addiction? A horn honk pulls him back to earth. He nods and starts the engine as his passenger door swings open with a cold rush of air. He recoils for an instant, but it's Nina. She drops into the passenger seat.

"Sorry," she says. "Did I scare you?"

"Yes. No." The car honks again. Davis waves it off and is rewarded with a middle finger.

Nina closes the door and hugs her big bag in her arms.

"No class?" he asks, making jazz hands. She shrugs, mimics his fluttering fingers—and she's five, in one of the scratchy tutus she lived in, directing him in her dance. He's wearing a pink tutu she put on his head like a crown and a sash she tied at his waist, and he's following her as she claps her hands, directing him, *step like this, like this*, prancing in the glittery ballet slippers he couldn't resist in a shop window near his worksite. Her delight that day made his whole life a success. *One, two, three. Yes, Daddy! Good Daddy!*

"Do you remember those ballet slip—"

"Red? With glitter!" She leans forward, like she's eager to remember too.

"I need to ask you about something." He turns off the engine and reaches in his pocket. "What are these?"

Her eyes widen on the bottle in his palm. Her body stiffens, she looks away, as if pretending not to see will make it disappear.

He sets the bottle on his console. "Tell me."

"It's not what you think. It's for work." And, as if warming to her denial, she says, "I'm under a lot of pressure, there's so much to do and sometimes, I get distracted." She points to the pill bottle. "They help me stay focused." She nods, as if convincing herself.

"And ... it keeps you from eating."

She slumps down into her seat.

"Honey." He searches for words to convince her that she needs help. "Everyone's afraid."

She frowns. "You're not," she says, defiantly.

He laughs.

"Dad?"

"I'm afraid of lots of things. Everyone's afraid of something." He relaxes back into his seat and exhales, realizing how tense he was; stunned that this simple truth telling could feel so good. They sit, watching the wind stir up the world outside. "So, little dancer. What frightens *you*?" he says, hoping she will trust him enough to tell him. Hoping he'll know what to say.

Wild Places

Every summer Toni's father took three weeks off from his milk route and piled her family into the station wagon for their annual camping trip. That summer of 1971 they headed to the Rockies. Toni's legs stuck to the plastic seat cover, and the endless drone of baseball on the radio made her queasy. Her two brothers stretched out in back with the gear while her twin sisters hogged the windows. Toni, the youngest, got the hump.

They'd just left Jackpot, Nevada, and crossed into Idaho when Dad turned down the game and said, "Listen up." He caught Toni's eye in the rearview mirror. "We have an announcement." He rested his arm along the back of the seat and squeezed Mother's shoulder. "We have another angel arriving in six months."

"Better be a boy," Jimmy grumbled. Joey agreed. Toni clapped, delighted to relinquish the unlucky position of baby and odd man out. The twins, Sheila and Sheyna, exchanged identical pinched faces. Mother didn't speak, just sat silent, staring from behind her dark glasses at the road ahead through the wild, desolate landscape. The license plate game fizzled without her. There were no rounds of "Row, Row, Row Your Boat."

★

On the second night in Yellowstone, Toni scrubbed out chili bowls, stuck with KP for cussing; bad language was reserved for her father's exclusive use. Bug bites itched under her sunburn after a day of aggravation on the river when her bathing suit ripped up the side. She'd tried to hold it together with safety pins, but eventually it just split to pieces. If her mother hadn't stayed behind in camp, she might have fixed it.

Dad stoked the campfire, peering past its flames to the darkness where Mom was "resting" in the car. Sheila and Sheyna argued over Crazy Eights at the wooden picnic table. Sheyna howled when Sheila pinched her arm and called her a cheater. Jimmy poked a flaming marshmallow at Joey, who swatted it, sending the burning stickiness—*smack*—into Dad's cheek. Dad cursed and swiped his face with the back of his hand.

"Knock it off," he yelled. "Boys, get firewood. Toni, see if Mom wants a s'more." Sheila and Sheyna just had to shut up. Dad settled in his chair and opened his first Oly with a fizzy gasp.

The whisper of music and the red glow of a cigarette led Toni to the car, where her mother sat staring at nothing, head back on the seat. Her cheekbones jutted. She'd been a sad blur at the edge of vacation. Toni tapped on the window, open a few inches, releasing Sinatra's moony song in cigarette smoke.

"Mom?"

Dad said it was the baby, but she'd been so sorrowful and strange Toni worried if it was something worse. She tapped again, but her mother didn't move.

"Mom!"

Her mother jumped, her empty eyes slowly focusing.

"Oh!" Toni said, legs weak with relief. The window cranked down to its stuck place, letting out more smoke and the stale plastic smell of the car. "Wanna s'more?" Toni asked, working her face into a sweet invitation.

Her mother looked past her. Toni followed her gaze to the twins arguing over cards, the dust cloud Jimmy and Joey made, and the sparks from the fire where Dad tossed another log. Her bandana slid back off her head, but she made no move to fix it.

"You eat one for me," she said, and patted Toni's cheek. Her hand smelled of Jergens and Newport menthol.

"Come sit by the fire," Toni urged. "It's real nice."

"I'm fine here, honey."

"I could sit with you?" Toni said, but got only a small smile of dismissal as her mother cranked the window closed.

At the fire, Toni climbed into her father's lap. He grunted, shifted her to his knee.

"You're double digits now, kiddo. Gettin' too big for my lap."

"Why won't she come out?" Toni asked.

Dad stared into the fire. "She's resting."

"But she hates that car."

He snorted. "I guess it improves with togetherness." He handed her a s'more. The grahams were stale but sweet and gooey with chocolate and marshmallow.

"S'good," Toni said, mouth full.

The boys debated player names for their imaginary baseball team as they unrolled sleeping bags on the dusty pads beside her parents' tent. The girls' tent had fallen apart the summer before, so they had two yellow tube tents; the twins shared one, Toni slept alone in the other. She blocked the ends to keep out spiders and bears, but by morning it was just a girl burrito, raining sweat.

"Where's Sheila and Sheyna?" she asked.

"Bathroom," Dad said.

Toni hated public bathrooms, especially campground toilets at night, and her sisters knew it. They liked to ditch her, and a few times ambushed her when she went alone. She hurried through the dark campground to catch up but saw them walking back, their hair wrapped in towels. She ducked behind a tree.

"Thanks a lot, assfaces," she hissed.

The bathroom door screeched open to the tang of damp metal, ammonia, and pee. No light. Something moaned. She aimed her flashlight inside fearing sharp claws would rip it away but saw a tall girl at the sink, her hair in a fancy braid. Toni had seen her at the river with her own folding chair, sunglasses, and a fluffy Beach Boys towel. She wore hoop earrings and a white bikini that showed she had boobs. Sheila and Sheyna had whispered about the girl and glared, but older boys ogled her like she was cherry pie à la mode.

Toni hurried into a stall, praying no spiders were under the seat. She always felt something sinister watching over the top or ready to grab her leg from under the next stall. Her mother said she peed like a horse and should try to tinkle, but she'd waited too long and wanted to finish before that girl left. When she came out, the girl was shining a flashlight into the sink.

"Don't use it," the girl said.

"Says who?"

"My ring fell down the drain. It's a gift from my mother. She's going to die." Toni pictured a woman, blond like the girl, clutching her chest and keeling over.

"What kinda ring?" The only ring Toni had really seen was the kind a man gave a wife.

"Opal," the girl said. "I'm a Scorpio." The flashlight made feathers of her lashes.

"Oh. I'm a Catholic."

The girl slumped back against the bathroom stall.

"Will you get in trouble?" Toni asked, wondering how she might be punished.

"What?" The girl's face screwed up like Sheila's when she said Toni was being a retard.

"Never mind."

"What am I going to do?"

No one ever asked Toni's advice.

"Don't worry," she said. "I know someone who can fix anything. I'll be right back."

Toni flew out the door, colliding with a mom clutching toothbrushes and kids in PJs.

"This bathroom," Toni said, arms flung wide to block the door, "is out of order." The woman had that fed-up-to-here look Toni's mother often wore, but she sighed and pulled her kids down the path to the next bathroom, giving up so easily. Toni ran.

Her mother still sat in the car; her dad still poked the fire. She collapsed against his chair, the one only he could sit in.

"Slow down," he said. "You're kicking up dust."

She squeezed the stitch in her side. "My friend dropped her sacred ring down the drain."

"What the hell are you talking about?" he asked, his whiskered face creased.

"We need your help. It's an emergency!" He grumbled, but he was drinking his Oly. "Bring your tool belt."

"What's going on?" Sheila asked. In the light from the kerosene lantern her face was green. She was curling Sheyna's long hair around empty orange juice cans. And they called Toni stupid.

"Everyone stay put," Dad ordered, but in his at-ease voice, so Jimmy and Joey followed, jumping, swatting at tree limbs, like a campground parade. Toni had to run to keep up.

"Go on." Dad jerked his head at the women's bathroom door. "Check the coast is clear." He drained his beer and chucked the can at the garbage bin. It kissed the rim and rolled onto the paper trash with a sigh.

Jimmy was only eleven months older than Joey, but much bigger; he hoisted Joey up to peek in the windows. "Hey!" Dad said and told them they'd better get back to camp or he'd knock them into the middle of next week. They ran off.

The girl was gone. Toni shone her light under the stalls, daring monsters to come out. This time she had her dad.

"All clear!"

A note in the sink read: *LOST RING. Please return to Janine, Campsite #39.*

Dad flicked the light switch up and frowned. He shone Toni's flashlight into the drain, then pulled a wrench from his tool belt and slid under the sink. She shivered, thinking of spiders, proud of his bravery.

"Hand me that," he said, pointing with the flashlight to a metal pail in the corner. He stuck it under the sink and gave Toni the light. His lips pursed as he tugged on the wrench. "Shine it on the pipe," he snapped, pulling hard with a grunt. Something squeaked, water trickled into the metal pail. *Ping!* "This what you're looking for?" Even in the dark bathroom it glittered, a tiny heaven of blue and green stars.

"Yeah! It's a ... opal?" She slipped it on her finger. "So we don't lose it," she explained when he raised his eyebrows. She'd never seen such a fancy thing up close. "C'mon!"

She pulled her father by his thick-fingered hand outside onto the cloverleaf road, searching with the flashlight for the small posts that bore each campsite's number. Peering in at the families they passed, she saw figures moving in nighttime rituals among the trees, faces floating white above campfires, people casting shadows on tent walls.

Toni heard the conversation and laughter before she got there. In campsite #39, light from smokeless lanterns and a roaring fire danced on the trees and shone off the sides of a silver Airstream trailer that looked like it was a hundred feet long. A gingham cloth covered a picnic table. Clothes hung short to long on a taut clothesline.

"Well, go on," he said.

"Come on, Dad," Toni said, and tugged him into the light of the campfire, ringed by folding chairs. It looked like they had company and were playing charades. Toni loved charades, but it always devolved into a riot of shouts, even punches, so Dad had issued a kill order until further notice.

The people looked like movie stars pretending to rough it. Their clothes were pressed and clean, and the mother wore pearl earrings. The campsite shone with newfangled gear. Even their ice chests were neatly labeled *Pop* and *Beer*. It was like a Holiday Inn of the forest. Toni had never stayed in a motel, but her Aunt Joanie sent postcards from her fancy Hawaiian vacations that her mom read while regarding Toni and her sibs as if they were too many unpaired socks.

"Can we help you?" Janine's dad's voice was deep. A Sears catalog man, tan in a blue polo shirt, his hair combed smooth with a part. He didn't stand, just studied them like he didn't know whether to get his camera or his gun.

"Is Janine here?" Toni asked.

"She's inside," the mother said. Her eyes surveyed Toni's feet, black with dirt, and her rumpled top stained with chocolate and mustard. Dad scratched his whiskers. The firelight made his flattop glisten and the scar on his cheek stand out. He wore checkered shorts and black socks with brown sandals, a look her mom had quit fighting. The mother smoothed her perfect blond flip. She raised her eyebrows at the other woman and called into the trailer for Janine. Toni was glad her mom wasn't there, eyes lifted like she was dreaming *Calgon, take me away* or thinking of the old boyfriend she spoke of sometimes.

Janine leaned out of the trailer. "What?"

"Ta-da!" Toni rushed to her; ring held high. "I found it! My dad got it out."

Janine shrieked and hugged her, whispering, "Thank you so much."

"You're welcome. I'm Toni," she whispered back, then snuck a peek inside the trailer, which had sofas, a tiny kitchen, bedrooms; Janine said it even had a closet bathroom.

"Then why go to the public one?"

"This one's just for emergencies," Janine explained.

"Okay, then," Dad said, and turned to go but Janine ran and wrapped herself around his arm.

"Thank you very much, sir," she said, looking up at him with her perfect face.

Sir? "All right, that's enough," Toni said, freeing her dad from Janine's grip.

"What's this?" asked the father, who stood and set a hand on his daughter's shoulder.

"I'm sorry, Daddy," Janine said, sounding like she might cry. "You told me to leave my ring at home, but I love it so much." She hugged his slim waist and grinned at Toni. *Daddy* lifted her hand; the ring caught the firelight. The mother, her smile big with love, explained to the other couple that the ring had been a cherished gift from her own mother, and she'd given it to Janine for her thirteenth birthday.

"It fell down the bathroom sink," Janine said. "This little girl's father saved it."

Little girl? Toni started to say it was all her idea, but Janine's father pulled out his wallet. Toni's father looked confused, then his jaw tightened, and Toni figured this guy was *a boss jerk who didn't know his ass from a hole in the ground.*

"Just being neighborly," Dad said, unsmiling. He shifted his tool belt on his shoulder and nodded to Janine's mother and friends. "You folks have a good night." He strode off through the trees. Janine's father shrugged. Toni could hear laughter and voices as she hurried to catch up, wishing that man had offered her the dough. Her dad was quiet on the walk back; he didn't take her hand. Toni chewed her thumb, worried he was mad.

Their campsite was dark and cluttered with bikes, fishing poles, jumbled cardboard boxes, and sagging tents. The only light came from the kerosene lantern abuzz with insects. She felt embarrassed and angry at once. Her mother still sat in the car. The fire smoked until her father threw on logs and it flared back to life. Toni sat on a stump pretending to read her Nancy Drew, stealing looks at her dad in his chair.

"Janine's not really my friend," she said. He just whittled a stick, working his jaw back and forth. Her mother stayed in the car. Toni didn't understand why he couldn't make her get out, or why she wouldn't just put on lipstick and sit with him and make tomorrow's plan.

Toni kept an eye on her father, staring into the fire like he'd lost something in the flames. When it was down to coals, he walked off and climbed into the driver's seat of the car. Toni tried to listen, but all she could hear was trees creaking in the wind. After a while her father got out, passed by without seeing her or telling her to go to bed, and crawled into his tent, alone.

She sat by the coals worrying, wondering what she could do to make her mom be herself again. Happy, like when they were home alone together, Toni beneath the board while her mother ironed as they listened to stories on the radio or Toni read aloud.

When the car rumbled to a start, Toni turned to see her mom driving away, the taillights quickly lost in the trees. She'd slipped off once before, earlier in the trip, but not at night. Toni hated not knowing where she was going or why. Her sisters' voices drew her into their tube.

"Mom left," she said, on all fours. "Where'd she go?"

"I don't know," Sheila said.

"Why would she just leave?" Toni asked, in a squeaky voice.

"Duh!" Sheyna said. "She's old. She doesn't want another baby. She's sick of kids."

"That's stupid." Toni punched her fist into the yellow plastic wall. "And a lie." A noise at her back startled her. She spun around, peering into the dark woods, certain something was watching. She shivered. "Hey," she said. "Can I sleep with you guys?"

No answer, just twin sounds of phony sleep.

"I know you're awake." She waited.

When they didn't answer, she crawled out of the stuffy tent onto the needled ground. The air was cool and sweet with pine. She crouched by the fire; a few coals glowed in the circle of stones, and she poked in pine needles that turned red, orange, white, then shriveled away.

"What are you doing?" Joey asked. He nudged Jimmy. They sat up in their sleeping bags, two buzzed heads white in the moonlight.

"You're gonna get it," Jimmy said.

She'd learned that zipped lips were safer than sass or a stuck-out tongue.

Joey, always full of big ideas, said, "Let's get this thing cookin'," and directed the gathering of needles. "Okay," he whispered, when satisfied with the pile's size. "On three. One," he mouthed, finger raised, "two," then, "three!" They rushed in and dumped armloads of needles on the coals. Toni feared they'd snuffed the fire out until a wisp of smoke snaked up. It trembled like they'd trapped a little critter, then *whoosh!* a towering flame shot skyward. She gasped and fell on her butt as the flames licked the overhanging pines. Dad flew out of his tent in his skivvies, eyes wild.

"Jesus Christ!" He hopped into shoes and dumped a thermos of Kool-Aid on the flames. Grape steam dirtied the air as he swung at the boys. "What the hell were you doing?" he shouted, but his sharp-eyed look shut them up. He told them to put the fire out "but good." They filled cups at the spigot and poured them on the fire ring until it became a small pond.

"Dammit," Dad yelled, "That's enough!"

"Jeez. Morons," Sheila said, wrestling her orange-juice cans through the tube opening beside Sheyna's matching metal head. "You almost burned down the forest."

Jimmy and Joey got in a fight over whose fault it was, earning them each a whack upside the head, which somehow made everyone easier and ready for bed. But Toni stayed by the fire. She couldn't sleep. Her bites itched. Their parking place was empty.

The boys whispered in their sleeping bags, pointing out stars. Toni crept over and squatted at Joey's side and told them about the hoity-toity people.

"The guy tried to pay Dad," she said.

"What's wrong with that?" Joey asked.

"He's a boss jerk," she said. "He made Dad mad."

Her brothers thought this over.

"We should get 'em," Jimmy said.

"Yeah," Joey whispered.

"We could slash their tires." Jimmy held up his Boy Scout knife he kept at the ready. "Injun style."

"Yeah, by the light of the moon," Joey said. "But Dad …"

"Yeah," Jimmy said, and burrowed into his bag.

"Well, I'm gonna do something," Toni said.

"Nah, you're too chicken," Joey said, and rolled over.

Toni pulled on her sweatshirt, grabbed her flashlight, snagged her father's knife from his chair, stuck it in her pocket, and marched out of camp, checking over her shoulder, but they didn't follow. She walked quickly along the road, the night much darker without her dad. But when she found the massive silver trailer, the camp was bright with moonlight, everything clean, like they'd swept the forest floor. She ducked and kept to the shadows. The ice chest squeaked as she opened it. She dropped to her knees, held her breath, checked the windows, but nothing moved.

She grabbed a cold bottle and ran into a ring of trees at the edge of the campsite where no one could see her. She squatted, her back pressed into the trunk of a Ponderosa pine and opened the bottle with the knife. It hissed, bubbles foaming over the top. She put her mouth to it, disappointed by the yeasty bitterness of beer. Still, she drank it, her booty, in rapid sips so cold she began to shiver. She pulled her sweatshirt down over her bent knees to her toes. She felt brave, imagining her brothers' awe when she told them. She turned her cheek to the Ponderosa's rough bark, sniffed its sweet vanilla. Her loud burp surprised her. She covered her mouth to stifle a laugh.

She pictured Janine wearing baby-doll pajamas, cozy in her own trailer bedroom, her parents sleeping together in the next room. It made her throat tight. She fingered her dad's knife, thinking about the way they'd upset him and about Jimmy's idea for vengeance. She opened the sharp blade and crept from her hiding place.

But standing beside the tire, she feared the loud bang like when their tire popped crossing into Wyoming and her mother cursed a startling, ugly word. Toni's eye fell on the clothes in the wind. She climbed an old stump and sawed at the cord until—*snap!*—it broke free and the long line of towels, tops, and bathing suits snaked on the wind, whipped at the trees, shuddered to the ground.

She stuck the bottle in her kangaroo pocket—proof—and walked back on a tilted road, the world dizzy. A rustling in the bushes startled her, and she remembered with a shudder the ranger who'd come through camp the day before to warn her dad about a mama bear with cubs.

She ran.

At the campsite, she found Jimmy and Joey sitting on one of the logs that marked the parking space. She showed them the bottle. Her brothers shared a look. Joey shook his head.

"Nah," he said. "You got it from the trash."

"Nuh-uh! Go see what I did." They didn't move. "Where's Mom?" she asked.

"She'll be back," Jimmy said.

"Yeah," Joey said, but he looked like he might cry.

Toni lay on top of her sleeping bag, woozy. The wind gusted harder, making the outside loud with strange noises that whispered something was coming while the picture part of her mind drew things the sounds might be. She wondered if a mother really could not want kids. Was there something about Toni—the last baby—that had hardened her mother's heart? Had she been that one last straw? She slid down inside her bag, the bottom gritty with camp dirt, and felt herself a pile of separate parts in need of retooling.

If she were an only child, her parents would be sleeping next door in their Airstream bedroom. She thought of Janine, safe, so beloved her mother gave her a special ring. She imagined Janine's mother horrified to find their clothes in the dirt. Then she thought of that trailer's closet bathroom and squeezed her eyes shut, willing herself to forget about it and fall asleep. No way was she going to the dark toilets alone.

The sound of the car made her gasp with relief. She hurried out to meet it. Lights flashed through the trees, coming closer. Toni stretched on tiptoe to see.

It was the ranger in his truck, his bright spotlight bouncing through the forest, searching for something wild, on the loose.

Save Me

When Hannah asked her punkabilly boyfriend to leave, he took his muttonchops, his electric guitar, and her bomber jacket. She wasn't the only thing he left behind in the third-floor apartment. At twenty-three Hannah felt weighty with possession. Fog beaded the windows as she studied a to-do list inspired by feng shui, the Chinese art of placement that promised happiness, clutter-free clarity, and good chi.

She drained her coffee, bitter without cream—he took that too—dragged her kitchen castoffs out to the building's exterior walkway and set them beside a growing pile of throwaways. Since hers was the end apartment on the top floor, she'd claimed the open walkway as her private deck with its view west to the sea. After purging him, she'd spent the weekend clearing junk from closets and drawers—detritus of the life she was shedding. Sometimes it seemed that's all she did.

A chill wind off the ocean ruffled the eucalyptus trees, releasing their cat pee stench. It pushed at the cardboard she wrestled to the deck. She secured one end with a Mexican planter and duck-walked the café table onto the cardboard, nearly smashing her toes. Her father's voice echoed from her childhood, "Where are your shoes?"

Her sister had found the metal table and two matching scrolled chairs at a garage sale and hired a man to drive the set from San Diego and hump it up Hannah's three flights of stairs. It needed muscled redemption, and the note taped to its marble top directed Hannah to paint it and use it on her deck. Caroline's gifts always came loaded.

Hannah rolled up the sleeves of a blouse her mother made, its floral pattern barely more than a memory. She put in her earbuds, flipped a rag over her shoulder, and pried open a can of black paint. The table wobbled, and she pressed her back under the top to lift it as she wedged a cardboard scrap beneath its pedestal base, now sanded clean. She dipped her brush, relishing the smooth exchange of bristles and paint. The metallic fumes transported her to her father's toolshed. Her sisters hadn't been interested in getting their hands dirty, and even Daniel hadn't seen the wonders of that shed. "Hannah's my odd duck," her father would say, a confused smile creasing his face. He had clear boundaries: women in the kitchen and tending children while men did "the work of this world." But she loved watching him at work, his deft hands and the short stub of his left index finger, which he called his reminder to be careful with saws. She would wait quietly for the crumb of a small task he might offer, sanding or separating nails. He was seventy-six now, and fitter than men half his age, but her family held his impending demise over her like a threat, for she alone by leaving the Church would bar his entrée to the Celestial Kingdom.

Her mother had called the day before to urge her, again, to come home. "Daddy's worried, honey." Hannah's head stormed with sound. "Now that that man is gone you can come back." Hannah could almost see her mother, hand cupped to her cheek like she'd been slapped. "Come home to the fold."

At work the previous Wednesday, Hannah's boss had announced the design firm's cash flow problem with a sorrowful shake of her head. She asked for volunteers to take time off without pay. Hannah's was the first hand up; she figured a four-day weekend would be enough time to give feng shui a chance.

She felt the vibration of someone's hurried footsteps, then the plodding steps of another. She tugged the earbuds from her ears. Hard heels sounded on the stairs. She sat up under the table and banged her head on its top.

"Shit!" She rubbed at the pain, adding black streaks to the pink strands in her blond hair. From under the table, she saw black pant legs and polished shoes. For a second, she thought cops, until she looked out to find a tall, slim man, another short and plump, both in white shirts and black ties. "Nobody's home," she said, and kept painting. They didn't leave. Hannah laid the brush across the paint can and crawled out.

"Good afternoon!" they said in unison with white-toothed smiles, the clouds' white perfection in a now blue sky reflected in their sunglasses.

Hannah sat back on her feet. "Twins?" she asked, running her eyes up the short man's black slacks and crisp white shirt and down the tall man's thin tie to his enormous black shoes.

"No, miss," said the short one, a moon-faced man-boy. "I'm Elder Pratt."

"You don't even look drinking age," Hannah said. The men exchanged a glance.

Elder Pratt's round face was plagued with acne. He tipped forward on the balls of his feet and said, "We'd like to bear testimony with you about our Lord, Jesus Christ."

"You're slipping. I've been here sixteen months, but you're only my second salvation visit."

"We won't take much of your time, miss."

"Ms. And my name's Hannah, but you probably know that."

"I'm Elder Bliss," said the tall one. He reminded Hannah of Daniel, with his blond hair, square jaw, and long-fingered hands.

"Elder Bliss. No first name?" When he didn't respond, she asked, "Is that a secret?" She knew they never used anything but Elder and their surname.

He looked at Elder Pratt, then said, "Moroni. Moroni Bliss."

"I'm so sorry," she said.

"For what?" Elder Pratt asked. The kid was almost a foot shorter than Bliss and constantly in motion, feet tapping, his dark head swiveling between them.

"Moron-I?" she said. "Middle school must have been brutal."

"I pronounced it Mor-O-nee back then," Elder Bliss said sheepishly. "But now I pronounce it as the Church prefers. Either way, I'm proud to bear the angel's name." His smile never wavered, and she felt an irrational pride in this Mormon man so well brought up. She looked off over the flat rooftops to the horizon, where fog lingered above the sea.

Pratt bounced on his feet. "Enjoying this beautiful Monday?"

Moroni pointed at the pile of junk and asked if she was moving. His haircut, fresh and close, glowed in the sunlight. When she didn't answer, he said, "I'm from Littleton, Colorado. Elder Pratt and I are students at BYU."

"What do you want?" Hannah asked, already knowing.

"We'd like to bear testimony about the Only True Church," Pratt said.

"You'd do better bearing lunch and a cold beer." She brushed her bangs from her eyes with the back of her hand.

"Hungry? I have a snack," Moroni said. He pulled a flattened breakfast bar from his shirt pocket. In spite of herself she laughed and took it.

"Goodies from home?" She peeled it open with her teeth, remembering the packages for Daniel's mission, how at sixteen she'd hidden messages in them that she hoped her mother wouldn't find, messages begging him to be true to himself and come home. She took a bite, suddenly ravenous.

Moroni squatted beside her and rubbed his large hands together, surveying her work. "I like restoring furniture, too."

Hannah rolled her eyes. She knew their instructions: *Find common ground.*

"Careful of the paint," she said.

Pratt bent, hands on knees, his fingernails bitten to nubs. "Elder Bliss," he said, "didn't you study furniture design last semester?"

"Yes."

Hannah reached across the deck to stuff the wrapper into a bag of papers, magazines, and her excruciatingly naked poems now in shreds. She dipped her brush in the paint and knelt beside the table's pedestal, the cardboard cool against her knees. Pratt's shoes tapped a staccato beat.

"Elder Pratt drinks too much coffee," she said, sweeping her brush along the sanded metal.

"He's energetic," Moroni said wearily, his eyes following her brush. "When do you rest?"

"Cocktail hour!" She grinned. He blushed, and she felt a twitch of guilt. He took his sunglasses off. His eyes were deep blue. "You remind me of my brother," she said. "Do you get homesick?" His eyes teared, surprising her.

Pratt said, "Surely you have a few minutes for our Savior."

"Or we can come back," Moroni said. "When you're not so busy."

Pratt disagreed in whispers Hannah couldn't make out.

"Okay," Pratt said. "Tomorrow? Ten a.m.?"

"You'd be wasting your time." Hannah put her earbuds back in to drown out their assurances of a return. She waited until the staircase stopped shaking with their retreat before peering through the metal bars to watch them go: one short, one tall, both in uniform. She had a flash of regret, then the familiar ache for her brother, and all she'd left behind. "Go with God," she called, something she'd picked up from the Catholics in college during her hunt for a new spiritual home: cold wooden pews, sickly incense, and a kiss of peace.

On Tuesday, Hannah woke feeling happier than she had in months. One more day before she'd be back at work. She put crisp new sheets on her bed and surveyed all she'd done, delighted by her uncluttered bedroom and polished floors, her gleaming, green-tiled bathroom purged of expired vitamins and useless beauty products.

Outside, the sky hung low and wet, holding back the sun. She stuffed the discarded shower curtain into a junk box gone soft in the damp. She shivered and hurried inside, where her heater hummed, filling her apartment with an aroma of burnt dust, teasing the eagle feather under Daniel's photo on her makeshift altar. Crows called outside the window. Each song she started on her iPod reminded her of home and things she wanted to forget; until she finally settled on ska.

At the small island between her living room and pocket kitchen she ate a quick breakfast—a hot dog bun with her mother's marmalade, long gone to sugar. She'd been waiting to shop until her world was clean and new.

When they came back for her, she was painting test squares on her freshly scrubbed walls. Elder Pratt knocked on her open door and stuck his pimply face in.

"Joy supreme," she said, her voice flat.

"Good afternoon, Hannah," Moroni replied, filling the doorway behind Pratt. His eyes swept the furniture bunched in the center of her living room. "You're a hard worker."

"No rest for the wicked," she said, surprised by her delight at seeing him. She leaned back and squinted at the mauve color she'd just painted. "Too dark." She opened another jar. "Maybe Eros Pink!" She waggled her eyebrows at Pratt and caught him looking at her breasts. He ducked his head. She felt sexy in pink shorts and a paint-splattered blouse tied above her trim waist. She dipped her sponge brush and painted a new square beside the first. "What do you think?" she asked. "Eros Pink or Zany Mauve?" She pointed to a jar on the counter. "I still have Cotton Candy."

"May I?" Pratt asked, motioning inside.

She shrugged, wondering why she was encouraging them. Pratt pushed the door wide, bumped her coffee table, and toppled a stack of books, upsetting a glass bowl filled with rose petals that fluttered to the floor.

"Oh, my heck!" Moroni hurried in after Pratt to help right the mess. They bonked heads, then staggered apart, their faces red. Hannah laughed. They were sweet. Moroni knelt to collect the petals in his lovely hands. "You sure like pink," he said, indicating the paint, her shorts, the streaks in her hair.

"It's feng shui. Pink is supposed to bring friendship and love to my life." Was she flirting? She'd read that feng shui could bring spiritual completeness too. She had nothing to lose.

"Well, it's working already," Moroni said. "We're friends, we're here, and the paint's not even dry." He smiled, eyes earnest and innocent, so like Daniel, who had been charming too when he was saving souls. Then she remembered his letters from his mission in Tahiti—staid, parroting the Church—they could have been written by anyone.

"Is that your family?" Pratt indicated the photo leaning on the couch. Four generations assembled around a large man squinting out of wire-rimmed glasses, a woman beside him smiling big with her mouth closed. Hannah wiped her hands on a rag and studied her clan. Daniel's high school graduation. In the picture her mother clutches his elbow while Hannah, fifteen, stands on his other side. Daniel's face in the picture is so like Moroni's. Her older sisters, all five married, all mothers, the oldest a grandmother, eyes trained on one child or another, lips frozen in an admonition, "Sit still" or "Say cheese." Men in a variety of shapes flank their women. Teenagers stand tall at the edges, and a girl beams into a father's face. A sea of toddlers sits at the feet of the group. "Yes, that's my family," Hannah said. "Mormons all. Save me." She pointed out her blond unsmiling self, her dark brows like a warning: This one does not belong.

"I have eight brothers and sisters," Pratt said. "Elder Bliss has six, just like you."

She picked up a desiccated rose petal by her foot and rubbed it between her fingers, a relic of a wedding that she, a Jack Mormon, was barred from attending.

"My mother sent these from my sister's wedding"— she pointed out Caroline in a long skirt and braid—"as a reminder to pray for love and marriage."

"That's real nice," Pratt said, his voice encouraging.

She shook her head, wondering why she'd saved them. She offered Moroni a waste bin and watched the rose petals fall from his hands.

"Is something burning?" he asked. She sniffed the air.

"It's my heater."

"You need a new filter," he said. "Let me change it for you."

Hannah scratched paint off the face of her watch. Clearly her letter to the Church hadn't changed a thing. She should throw the boys out, she was only raising their hopes of a victory, but she pulled a scratchy new filter from her closet, drawing courage from the order she found there. Moroni opened the heater knowing just what to do. He even vacuumed the dust.

Outside, she propped the filthy filter against the pile of junk. Pickup was that afternoon, and she longed to see it all crushed in the garbage truck and carted off. Moroni followed her out. She thanked him, reminding herself he was just following protocol—*be helpful*—so that he could have his way with her soul. He looked into her eyes as if reading her struggle. Crows fought for purchase on the deck's metal railing.

She knelt by the café set, testing whether it was dry, opened the can of black paint, and stirred. Pratt came out, hands shoved into his pockets.

"You're a multitasker," Moroni said as the sun finally broke through the fog.

"I took time off without pay," Hannah said. "I don't plan to waste it." Her father believed in doing one job at a time, but since Saturday she'd been a whirlwind of industry, sorting what to keep, what to throw away, cleaning, making repairs, each task inspiring another.

"Surely," Pratt said, "we can take a few minutes for Heavenly Father."

Hannah squinted up at him, moving her head so his body blocked the sun. "My family sent you, didn't they?"

"It's our mission," he said. "We go where Heavenly Father calls."

"He called you to San Luis Obispo? To the Seaward Shores? To Unit 305?"

He nodded.

She began slapping the paint on. Tiny black flecks speckled her knees. "I suppose you didn't see the landlord's sign: No Solicitations."

Moroni smiled and spread his hands. "We're not selling, just sharing the word of God."

"Does it really matter," Pratt asked, "how Heavenly Father finds you?"

Hannah started on one of the chairs, thinking. Thinking of the Church, the sense of goodness and purity, the comforting belief that there was order to life, that everything did have its place.

"You're lucky," she told them.

"Why?" Pratt asked.

"Having no doubts. Life's questions and answers taken care of"—she snapped her fingers—"just like that."

Moroni studied his boat-like shoes.

"I'm on your ExMorm reclamation list," Hannah said. "That's why you're here. It's not my first visit. Won't be the last."

They shared a look.

"It's normal to doubt," Pratt said, watching Hannah paint. "I once strayed to the Baptists, but I came home to"—he raised a finger to heaven—"the One True Church."

"Well, doubt's what I do best." She waved the brush as she spoke, flicking paint on the cardboard and deck. "That's what being a grownup is, living in the question." She hastily finished the chair, set the brush down, strode into her apartment, and slammed the door.

In the kitchen sink, she scrubbed paint from her fingers, the tips raw from cleaning and scraping. *Should have worn gloves*, but gloves made it difficult to maintain a firm grip. She drank a glass of water, then dug in her cookie jar for cigarettes. Another thing her ex left behind: a bad habit. She lit one, pulling the noxious air into her lungs to give her backbone. Outside, she exhaled a long white stream into the bright sky and leaned her back against the railing, watching her reflection smoke in her apartment window.

Pratt gripped the railing and lifted his chin. "Tobacco," he preached, "is not for the body, and is not good for man, but an herb for bruises and sick cattle. It's an addiction."

"And that, Elder Pratt," Hannah said, pointing her cigarette at him, "is why I'd never make it in the Celestial Kingdom. Spend eternity with nonsmoking, nondrinking folk? I don't think so. Besides, I'm not addicted."

"I am," Pratt said, and puffed out his chest with obvious pride. "I'm addicted to Scripture."

Hannah raised her eyebrows at Moroni who fought back a smile.

"And Pepsi," Moroni added.

Pratt ignored him. "I'm addicted to Heavenly Father. He makes me healthier, happier."

"Good for you," Hannah said.

"I'd like to bear testimony with you."

She flicked her ash over the rail. "I have my own path."

Pratt's acne-inflamed face grew even redder; he dropped his chin like a bull preparing to charge. Moroni reached out and patted Pratt's arm. Pratt flinched like he'd been shocked.

"Don't!" He gave Moroni a look of disgust. "Hannah," he said, "you can paint your hair and walls pink, but—"

He stopped, distracted by footsteps up the stairs. A wiener dog appeared, yipping at the air.

"Caroline," Hannah groaned. "Just what this party needs."

A blond in impossibly high heels staggered up the last two stairs. She wore red lipstick, a low-cut peasant blouse, and very tight jeans. "Hey! You need an elevator." Her eyes lit up when she saw the two men.

"Meet the salvation squad," Hannah said.

"Well, save me," Caroline said, wide-eyed, as if the missionaries were a surprise. She pointed at the trash piled on the walkway outside Rachel's apartment. "What's all this?" Her dog sniffed the shower curtain, then lifted his short leg and peed.

"Gosh, that's helpful," Hannah said.

Caroline bent to scold her dog, giving the boys a closeup view of her breasts. Hannah couldn't help being amused when Pratt nearly fell in. "This is Deville," Caroline said, petting the dog with an indulgent smile. "I named him that because he's such a devil." She asked for a smoke and pointed at the table, gleaming in the sunlight. "Resurrection!" She laughed, alone. She played perfect

Miss Mormon at home, but on her own she had a good old time. Hannah snuffed out her cigarette in the Mexican planter with its waterlogged skeleton of a fern.

"Take them." Hannah handed the pack to her sister. "One more thing I don't need."

Pratt beamed, then frowned as Caroline lit up. Caroline scanned Pratt's pitted face, Moroni's blond good looks, and the badges over their hearts. Hannah felt sorry for Pratt, who was squirming, his eyes fighting a losing battle, helpless before Caroline's curvy, sanctimonious sexiness. There had been talk surrounding Caroline's mission, rumors of partying, bad behavior with men.

Hannah grabbed her brush, eager for distance. She still had the living room to paint.

Caroline's eyes, rimmed in kohl, thick with mascara, took their time over Moroni. "You're so tall. You must be an athlete." He took a step back.

"Leave him alone," Hannah said, startled by Moroni's discomfort and her impulse to rescue. "How's Ronald?"

Caroline pinched her lips, clearly annoyed by the mention of the uptight Mr. Mormon man she'd married for money. "In Brazil, working, of course."

"Why the surprise visit? And how'd you get your holy underwear on under that outfit?"

"I promised Mom I'd deliver this stuff on my way home." She set a paper bag down and pulled out jars of preserves and sacrament cards. "I stayed with them for ten days!" An accusation. "And that drive is hot," she said, as if this excused her violation of Church law.

"I'm glad to meet you, miss," Pratt said.

Caroline flashed him a flirty smile as she handed Hannah something wrapped in a tea towel. "Mom was throwing this out. I thought you'd want it."

Hannah put down her brush and pulled off the towel to find the Elvis clock she'd given Daniel on his thirteenth birthday, when the truth was still safely hidden. She carried it inside, found a battery in her very tidy utility drawer, and hung it on a naked nail above the squares of pink paint. She watched Elvis's legs swing back and forth in time.

"He's got too much girl in him," her father said. Oh, they'd loved him, but their love smacked up against the Temple walls and its inlaid stones. Daniel confided in her just before his sixteenth birthday party. "Have you told Mom and Dad?" she asked in a whisper, her face turned away to hide her shock. "I'm too ashamed," he said, his chin trembling. She wrapped her arms around him and offered support as she'd been taught, "Let's pray for Heavenly Father's guidance." Later, worried about Daniel, she told Caroline, who curled her nose as if Daniel was a smell she couldn't abide. Hannah remembered again with a familiar ache in her belly that it was Caroline who'd insisted Daniel go to the Bishop, who'd sent him to a church therapist, who'd instructed him to suppress desire, suppress himself.

Outside, she heard Pratt ask Caroline, "Are you staying long?"

Hannah leaned out her door and said, "She's leaving very soon."

"I'd like to bear witness with you, Caroline," Pratt said. Caroline looked as if he'd said something nasty and pushed past Hannah into the apartment, dragging Deville by the leash.

Pratt turned crimson.

"Deville better not pee in here!" Hannah warned. The bathroom door slammed.

Pratt stepped inside. "Where did you ladies grow up?"

"Utah. Look," Hannah said, as Moroni came in. "I tried the Mormon way. I was a square peg. I try to forget all that. Talk to Caroline; she's one of you—when it suits." She knew these missionary visits would never end. Her mother would make sure of that.

"Don't you have some positive memories of home, of the Church," Moroni asked, his eyes urging her to cooperate. Caroline reappeared, perched on the arm of the couch and flipped through Hannah's feng shui book. Hannah wanted to rip it from her hands but spread newspaper over her kitchen counter instead and taped it down tight. She opened Cotton Candy and dipped a new sponge brush, remembering her mother with the sudden pang of homesickness that hit her hard at times— decorating tiny chairs for baby gifts, at the sewing machine making matching Temple dresses, in the kitchen baking her famous cinnamon rolls.

Pratt said, "I can't believe there weren't good times." Hannah felt Caroline watching.

"Sure,' she said and painted a new pink square under Elvis's legs.

"And what about the Church?" Pratt asked.

All those Sundays, all the weddings she was barred from. Hannah scowled. Moroni leaned against her open door, his face expectant. And she remembered.

"There was this one Sunday ... I was six, maybe seven. Leaving church, the doors opened on this rainbow—a double rainbow." She looked out the window to where the sun was painting the clouds crimson in a baby blue sky. "I can still see those colors." She turned the sponge brush in her fingers. "Incredible." Paint dripped on her toe. "My father squeezed my hand and I felt something ... I don't know, like a shivering in the air." She laughed. "I think I expected God to leap from the clouds in a chariot with silver horses."

Moroni said, "Heavenly Father was rewarding your worship with His bounty."

"Maybe." Hannah bent and wiped her toe, remembering the whole congregation spilling out of the church under that magnificent sky. Was that the last time she'd been certain, the last time she'd belonged? Now the late afternoon sun through the door, on the missionaries' white shirts, reminded her of another Sunday, fifteen and alone on the steps outside the Temple. Snow covered the plaza, the frozen fountain, stretching like a white sheet to the snow topped mountains. She'd shivered in a red dress, her silent protest, barred from another wedding because she couldn't believe.

"Why can't you just focus on that?" Caroline asked. "Be thankful, rejoin the Church, make everyone happy?" As if it could be that simple.

Hannah stepped back to compare the colors. "What? Live your lie?"

"You make everything so complicated!" Caroline snapped.

The *tick-kick, tick-kick* of Elvis's legs was the only sound. Hannah remembered Daniel, imitating The King, skinny legs jerking, head swinging, crooning into a carrot microphone: *You ain't nothin' but a hound dog.* Oh, Daniel. The night they came for him she was alone in her room. Lights swung across her wall as a truck came up the drive. Was Moroni her punishment, so like him, coming here now?

She took in the chaotic state of her living room. "I feel sick."

"That is the Holy Ghost telling you our message is true," Pratt said.

"They took my brother to a conversion camp in Colorado. Reparative therapy," Hannah said, making zapping motions with her fingers.

Moroni flinched.

"They did that because Jesus loves him," Pratt said.

"Hannah!" Caroline said. "You're not supposed to—"

"Why? Because it's true?" Hannah glared at Caroline. "How can you live with that?"

"They thought it was for the best." Caroline swiped at her eyes, smearing her mascara.

Hannah stared at her in disbelief. "Best for who? You? Your Church? Not for Daniel."

"It's your Church, too," Caroline said.

"No. Not anymore." She tilted her head. "Why are you here?"

Caroline's eyes flicked around the room as if she were surprised to find herself there. She stood. "I should go." Her lower lip quivered. "You just keep making life hard, throwing your family away, see where that gets you." She pushed past the missionaries to the deck, Deville barking as they walked down the steps. Hannah fought the urge to stop her. Moroni turned his back to her in the doorway and watched Caroline descend.

Pratt pointed, sweat rings bloomed under his arms. "Should I go after her?"

"You really want to help?" Hannah said. "Make the Church accept my Resignation Letter." She reached up to her shelf, between Buddha and St. Francis, for the Book of Mormon. She slid the letter from its pages denying her request to leave the Church. Pratt eyed it warily. Hannah spoke to Moroni's back. "They tell me I'm too young, 'a little lost right now.'" Her lips tingled. She shook the letter at Pratt, remembering Daniel's face the night they took him, terrified, sandwiched between two men, looking out the rear window. "I should have stopped them." Pratt started to speak, but Hannah cut him off. "If it weren't for them, I'd still have my brother. You all use that thing like a bludgeon," she said, thrusting a finger at the Book of Mormon pressed to Pratt's chest.

She pointed to Daniel's picture and said softly, "That's my beautiful brother."

"Next to the crime of murder is the sin of sexual impurity." Pratt nodded to Moroni.

"Don't," Moroni said and turned around.

Hannah looked between the two men. "Did they punish you?" she asked Moroni.

He blinked, looked away. "Pardon?"

"Oh. God," she said.

Pratt straightened his tie. "He chooses not to act on his unholy desire."

"Right," Hannah said, her breathing tight. She paced back and forth. She still had Daniel's letter, so terse, so unlike him, no return address. "He wanted me to forget that I knew. But I couldn't. They wouldn't tell me where he was. I couldn't even write." She sat down on the edge of her sofa.

"The devil taunts many men, that's how he works. He taunted your brother, but the Church healed him. Now he's saved." Pratt's eyes were intense. "You'll see in time that it's the right thing." He opened his book, smoothed the left page, then the right.

"He killed himself three years ago," Hannah said.

Elvis twitched on the wall. Moroni stood shoulders hunched, hands clasped behind him. She thought of playing hide-and-seek with Daniel, how she'd delighted in finding his hiding place, sneaking up, leaping on his back, laughing as he pretended to throw her off, as he raced for the safe base, though he'd already been tagged.

"Maybe we should come back," Pratt said, bouncing on his feet, "when you're not so—upset. I can help you understand—"

"Just get the fuck out." The lump in her throat infuriated her.

"Why would you want to let go of Heavenly Father?" Moroni asked, looking miserable. "Without Him, without your family, you'll always be alone."

Garbage trucks rumbled in the parking lot below. Her pile of trash still huddled on her deck, huge in the last light.

"Let us pray," Pratt said. "To ease your suffering. Then we'll go."

Moroni clutched her hand in his, strong and warm. She started to pull it away but closed her eyes and let the words rush over her, familiar, like her mother's touch. She took a deep breath, remembering Sunday afternoons, hide-and-seek with Daniel, cooking with her sisters, her mother so joyful after church, her father more expansive than at any other time of the week.

She looked down at Moroni's hand holding hers, the crisp cuff of his white sleeve ruined now with her pink paint.

Acknowledgments

Grateful acknowledgement is made to the following publications in which these stories first appeared:

- "Abundance" in *Mid-American Review* – Finalist for the Sherwood Anderson 2018-2019 Fiction Award
- "Wild Places" in *Alaska Quarterly Review*
- "Magic Fingers" in *Dogwood: A Journal of Poetry and Prose*
- "Save Me" – Finalist for the Eric Hoffer Award in *Best New Writing*
- "War Paint" in *New Millennium Writings* – Winner of the NMW 53rd Annual Writing Award
- "A Hard Man to Find" in *A Courtship of Winds*
- "Where Are You, Really?" in *Northwind Magazine*
- "Finger Food" in *Lynx Eye*
- "Lilies" in *Stone's Thrown Magazine*
- "Wake" in *Thin Air Journal*
- "A Whole Hand" in *The Madison Review*.

Special thanks to Hedgebrook and the Vermont Studio Center where I had the privilege of space and time to hone these pieces.

Gratitude

I am indebted to Matt Potter for his belief in this book and his support of my work over the years. His editorial expertise and attention to detail made this collection better.

I am blessed by brilliant literary traveling companions who patiently read my writing: Laura Miller, Mary Volmer, Anne Helmstadter, Rebecca Brams, Kaija Langley, and my ArmadillHers—Jody Hobbs-Hesler, Susan Baller Shepard, Charmaine Wilkerson—who remind me that creatives require tough outer shells and soft underbellies.

Thank you to Leslie Shown and Joan Marie Wood who gave me permission at the beginning.

The stories in this collection are stronger for feedback from wise editors and inspiring teachers, including St. Mary's College Creative Writing Program where a few of these stories had their beginnings.

I am forever grateful to "Mc", Kevin McIlvoy, an extraordinary teacher, and a singular human being, who helped me believe in my voice and trust that my stories have a place in this world. He was taken too soon and is forever missed.

My deepest thanks to my husband, Andy, whose unfailing support helped make this book possible.

To my beautiful sons, my joy, Sam and Aaron, for always cheering me on.

Also from Truth Serum Press

truthserumpress.net/catalogue/

- *Where the Wind Blows* by Sandra Arnold
978-1-923000-22-3 (paperback) 978-1-923000-26-1 (ePub)
- *Love, Lemons and Illicit Sex* by Nod Ghosh
978-1-923000-06-3 (paperback) 978-1-923000-09-4 (ePub)
- *Remembering the Dead* by Lewis Woolston
978-1-922427-58-8 (paperback) 978-1-922427-62-5 (ePub)

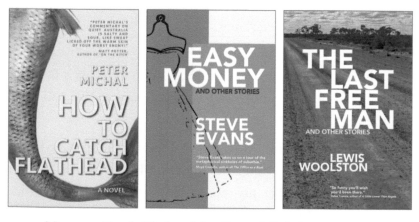

- *How to Catch Flathead* by Peter Michal
978-1-925536-94-2 (paperback) 978-1-925536-95-9 (ePub)
- *Easy Money* by Steve Evans
978-1-925536-81-2 (paperback) 978-1-925536-82-9 (ePub)
- *The Last Free Man* by Lewis Woolston
978-1-925536-88-1 (paperback) 978-1-925536-89-8 (ePub)